The Neighbor

F.A. Witte

THE NEIGHBOR

First edition. April 24, 2023.

Copyright © 2023 F. A. Witte.

ISBN: 979-8215795118

Written by F. A. Witte.

Dedication

To my Itsy, Claudia and my Prince, Malakai. You two have brought me so much happiness. I hope you both follow your heart and dreams no matter what they may be. I love you both to the moon and back. Always and forever my loves.

Chapter One

Krystian

"What should we do this weekend?" I asked Andrea, my girlfriend of three years now. She sat beside me on the couch in my living room. My mom was in the kitchen wrapping up dinner. I wasn't sure what she was making but it sure smelled good.

"We can go to the movies." she suggested. Movies were always her go-to thing to do. I wasn't into it very much. I only went to please her.

"Yeah, sure, that sounds like fun." I lied. I kissed her forehead. She loved it when I did that. Her bleach blonde hair fell in her face like it usually did, so I pushed it behind her ear. She looked at me and smiled.

"You are always so sweet to me." Her cheeks grew red.

"You're my everything." I told her. I leaned in to kiss her but was rudely interrupted by my mother announcing dinner was ready.

"You kids come eat!" She yelled from the kitchen. Andrea just smiled at me before jumping up from the couch. She reached her hand out for mine. I grabbed hers, and she pulled me up.

THE NEIGHBOR

The kitchen table only had a place set for three. I was still getting used to the fact that there was only me and my mom left. My dad left us about six months ago after my older brother, Kameron, was murdered a year ago. My mom and dad blamed each other, even though it was neither of their faults. Some crazed murderer killed him, and another local kid named Samuel. They never found the guy but with the anniversary of the deaths coming up, the whole town has been in a frenzy, and they all want answers. Some think it was the local hermit, George. Some believe it was just a person passing through and no telling where he could be now. I didn't know what to believe. The only thing I knew for sure is I lost a brother and my best friend. Some days were still hard to deal with, others, I had Andrea to keep my mind off the negative things.

My mom used a steak knife and fork to cut into her pork chop. Before taking a bite, she dipped the piece of meat into her mashed potatoes and scooped up a small amount. I couldn't help but smile at her actions. Kameron used to do the same thing.

"How is dinner?" she asked when she was done chewing.

"Dinner is delicious like always, Ms. Everett." Andrea said in her soft voice. "I always love your cooking."

"I like the flavor." I added. "Did you try something new?" I knew complimenting her on her cooking would make her feel good. I wanted to see her smile. She hardly smiled anymore. Ever since our world fell apart.

"I did actually," she seemed happy to know that I noticed. "It's something I had seen on a cooking show."

"I'm going to have to get the recipe from you so I can give it to my mom." Andrea said before taking a bite of her peas.

"Remind me before you leave." My mother responded to her. Andrea nodded. "So, we are getting new neighbors." My mom said to change the subject.

"I saw the moving trucks when I got here." Andrea sounded overly excited.

"Hopefully not a bunch of weirdos." I stated.

"Maybe they'll have some kids your age, Krystian." She looked at me with a smirk. "It would be good for you to make some friends."

"I have friends, mom." I reminded her.

"I didn't mean it that way, but a few more wouldn't hurt." She was defensive.

"What I need is out of this house." I blurted out. Andrea looked at me shocked and then looked at my mom, waiting for her response.

"What are you talking about, Krystian?" She looked confused. "You leave the house all the time."

"Not since Kameron died!" I shouted. "I feel like I'm locked in a prison. I go to school and come home. On occasion I get to take my girlfriend to the movies. It's not fair at all."

THE NEIGHBOR

"Krystian!" Andrea said my name in shock at what I had said. My mom just looked at me with her eyes watering up. We all sat at the table not touching our food, just staring at it. I regretted what I said instantly. My mood has been so out of control lately. I wanted answers about Kameron's death, and I grew angry every day that I didn't get them. I shouldn't take it out on my mom. I know she didn't do it. But she took his death out on me as well. I had to live like I was next or something. Like the same thing was going to happen to me as well. She was paranoid. She did lose a son but that was no excuse to try to keep me prisoner in this house. I wanted to go do things with my friends and hang out. I should be able to walk out my front door and not have to sneak out the window to do so. I wanted to be a teenager and live life.

The silence grew awkward, and I knew I had to say something. "Mom, I'm sorry, I knew I shouldn't have said anything." I apologized. She didn't respond. Instead, she wiped the tear that escaped her eye. She stood up from her seat and grabbed her plate that was barely eaten. She walked to the trash can and scraped her food into the trash.

"Mom?" I called her, but she still ignored me while she placed her plate gently in the sink.

"Ms. Everett?" Andrea tried to get her to respond. But it was a failed attempt.

"Mom, I said I was sorry." I felt like a total fool. I upset my mom and now she wouldn't even talk to me. The look on her face told me she was more heartbroken than angry. She always went quiet when she was sad. She hardly talked at all during the divorce with my dad. Maybe if she talked to him, they could have worked out their differences. My dad would yell at her all the time. He blamed her for Kameron sneaking out of the house that night. He was working overnights on the oil rig and Mom and Kameron had a disagreement over Debbie, Kameron's girlfriend at the time. He wanted to take her out for their anniversary and Mom wouldn't let him use the car. He stormed out of the house and that was the last any of us ever saw him. It destroyed my mom. My dad only made the situation worse, until he finally filed for divorce. She was just getting back to her normal self, talking more and trying to make friends. I was proud of her, but I didn't like the way I was being treated. I had the choice of living with my dad, but I knew she needed me. I couldn't leave her in this house alone.

"Nice going, Krystian." Andrea was upset with me as well.

"I said I was sorry." I put my head down in shame.

"That's still not a good enough excuse for saying what you did." She scolded me.

"So, I should leave it all bottled up inside?" I was upset she was taking my mom's side. She obviously didn't understand what I was being put through. Then again, how could she? She only came over twice a week to spend time with me. We see each other every day at school. That just wasn't enough for me. But I loved her and let her spend time with her friends like she wanted.

"No Krystian. Don't leave it bottled up inside. There is always a place and time, and this just wasn't the right time. At least not how you said it. Your mom had to bury her son and she lost her husband in the process. Geez Krystian. Tear her heart out why don't you."

Andrea made me feel more like a jerk. I knew I had to have a talk with my mom, but I wanted to give her time to calm down first. Dinner was pretty much ruined. None of us ate another bite.

"I have something for you in my room." I told Andrea, remembering the gift I ordered for her online. I couldn't do real shopping. Ever since what happened to Kameron, all my shopping was mostly online unless my mom or dad were with me. I got to hang out with my dad every other weekend, but he wasn't the shopping type. I never thought I was either until I couldn't do it.

Andrea smiled big. "What is it?" she asked excitedly.

"You're just going to have to wait and see." I taunted her. She loved surprises and I wanted her to wonder.

"Well, what are we waiting for? Let's go!" She led the way upstairs to my room leaving our plates still on the table.

As soon as she entered my room, I grabbed her waist and turned her around to face me. I kissed her hard and passionately. I was in love with her. She had her flaws just like me, but I could never picture being with anyone else besides her. She pulled away from me and whispered. "I love you, Krystian."

"I love you too." I said, staring into her brown eyes. Her bleach blonde hair was in her face again and I brushed it gently behind her ear. She smiled at me. Her smile made me melt.

"Where is it?" she blurted out. I ignored her and started tickling her.

"Stop! Krystian!" She laughed so hard. "You are going to make me pee myself." I stopped tickling her and she went to sit on my bed. I walked over to my dresser drawer and pulled out a little black box that held a silver locket with a picture of us tucked inside. She was always mushy about things like that.

"Oh, my goodness Krystian, you bought me jewelry?" she said as she saw the black box in my hand. I just smiled at her. She bounced up and down on my bed with excitement. The big smile on her face made my day. She grabbed the box out of my hand and opened it. Her eyes started to water when she saw what was inside. "It's beautiful, Krystian."

"Open it up." I told her. I was excited to see her face when she saw our photo. Andrea pulled the locket out of the box and slowly opened it up.

She gasped when she saw the picture inside. "I love it, Krystian."

I wiped the single tear that was rolling down her tan face and kissed her cheek gently. I knew she loved the gift by the way she kissed me after that.

THE NEIGHBOR

"Put it on me please." She asked.

"Of course." I told her. I would do anything for her.

"I love you so much, Krystian Lopez." She smiled ear to ear, and I knew she was telling the truth.

"And I love you so much, Andrea Stewart." We kissed once more. Andrea didn't realize that she was the one who saved me. After Kameron's death I almost lost it, but she was there for me like no one has ever been. She understood my pain. She lost her dad a couple of years before Kameron's death, but Mr. Stewart committed suicide. I helped her get through that loss and ever since then we have been inseparable. With just her mom and two older brothers all working hard to keep their house, she wasn't spoiled like she used to be. She had to give a lot of things up and I knew anything from me would put a smile on her face. I didn't want to get her just anything though. I wanted her to have the world, but I couldn't afford the world. When I saw the locket online, I knew she was going to love it. And the picture of us was when we first became official three years ago.

A knock on the door startled us both. "I need to go to the store," my mom's voice interrupted us. "Would you two like to go?"

Andrea and I both looked at each other confused. She must not be upset anymore.

"Actually, I need to get going." Andrea spoke up. "You two go. I'm sure you have a lot to talk about."

My mom smiled at her and nodded her head. "I'll walk you out." I told Andrea. I held her hand as we walked out the front door and down the steps of my front porch. Mom noticed the new neighbors walking out to their car. She waved at them, and they kindly waved back. I kissed Andrea on her forehead.

"I'll call you later." I whispered in her ear.

"You better!" She replied and walked off down the street. She only lived a couple of streets down from me. I usually walk her home but here lately I haven't been allowed. That's my life. I can't even walk my own girlfriend home.

Chapter Two

Kora

I looked outside the car window from the backseat of my dad's piece of crap red 2005 Explorer. We were almost to our destination: Willow Creek. A small town in the middle of nowhere in Arizona. I hated my parents for disrupting my life and forcing me to move here. Dad lost his job, so they decided to spend their life savings in a café two hundred miles from home, which used to be Phoenix. I only had one friend back home and that was Terra. Terra was unique, just like me. We were the outcasts of our school. "The weirdos" is what the popular kids called us. Except in Phoenix, we were a team. We had each other's backs no matter what. Now I'm going to be alone here. I didn't know how the teenagers here acted. I didn't know what to expect from this town at all. Terra wasn't going to be here to get me through what might happen.

We pulled off the highway into a residential area. All the houses looked nice. I wondered which one was going to be our new home.

"Almost there." My mother announced from the passenger seat. I looked at her and rolled my eyes. "Kora, stop!" She said to me.

"Once you get settled in you are really going to like it." My dad tried to convince me.

"Whatever you say." I mumbled under my breath as I rolled my eyes once again. They didn't know what they were talking about. I liked where we were before. Our old home and my friend Terra. My parents just didn't understand how this move has affected me.

"Look at it as a fresh new start. Nobody knows you here and you can be anyone you want to be."

"Seriously Mom? I don't want to be anything but myself. When are you going to accept who I am?" I couldn't believe she said that to me. It was like she didn't even like me. She looked at me shocked as she struggled to come up with something to say.

"That's not what your mother means, Kora. Stop taking this so personal." My dad jumped to her defense.

"Then what does she mean?" I argued.

"It means everything that happened at your last school is in the past now. Don't let it affect you here." My dad said. My mother looked at him and smiled with relief. He said exactly what she wanted to say but couldn't.

"We love you Kora and just want the best for you. We have heard such good things about Willow Creek and think you will be just fine here." My mother added.

"Like I said before. Whatever!" I still wasn't convinced this town would be anything different from Phoenix.

We turned onto Dixie Avenue. The street name made me chuckle. This place had some funny street names. The houses on this street looked even nicer than the others we passed. My dad pulled into the driveway of a two-story, half brick house. The bottom half was brick with a white wrap-around porch, and the top half had light blue siding. The garage was also brick with a light blue garage door. I noticed the front door was red. I had never seen one painted red before. They were usually all white. I wondered if I could get my parents to change it. The red door with the brick and blue siding just didn't sit well with me. Other than that, I really liked it, it was big, but I wasn't ready to admit that to them just yet.

"How did you guys afford something like this?" I asked.

"It was on the market for a while, so we talked them down on the closing cost." My dad answered.

"Isn't it lovely?" my mother asked me.

"It looks alright," I told her. "I have to see the inside first."

"Stop being so negative, Kora. You are really going to like it here. I promise." My dad told me. I ignored him. I unbuckled my seat belt and climbed out of the car. The movers were already at the house unloading all our furniture. Mom got distracted by two of the movers almost dropping her dresser. I laughed at how she overreacted. She jumped out of the car screaming at them to stop. I hoped they did drop it. Dad was already exploring the garage. I glanced around the neighborhood I was now officially a part of and wondered what the people would be like. Would I make new friends? My mom said I can be somebody new. Who could I be? The popular girl maybe? I burst out laughing with that thought.

"Go check out your new room." My dad shouted to me from the garage.

"Okay Dad." I shouted back. I walked around some movers to get into the house. As soon as I walked into the house, the first thing I saw was the stairs. I decided to check out the bottom half of the house first. I walked to my left and there was a big living room with a fireplace. I knew Mom picked this place because of the fireplace. She was fascinated with them. Instead of the usual red brick fireplace, this one was gray brick with a bookshelf on each end of it. I gave mom props for this one. It really looked gorgeous. The black shelves really made it stand out.

I walked into the kitchen that looked spacious. Way too big for a family of three. Mom loved to cook, and the island stove was perfect for her. The walls were a light gray with white trim. I liked it.

I grew excited thinking about what my new room looked like. Before I headed upstairs to find out I finished adventuring downstairs. I found a closet and a bathroom. I ran up the stairs almost knocking one of the movers down.

"Watch where you're running!" He yelled at me. I didn't look back or respond to him, I just kept running up the stairs to my new room.

I opened the first door I saw. After looking inside, I already knew this was my room. Not overly big but just the right size. My belongings were already along the wall next to a big window. The window was the only thing I disliked. The closet had more than enough space for my things. This was the first time I felt excited about the move. I looked out the window with a smile on my face. The first real smile I had in a long time. I noticed the neighbor's house directly in front of me. That may be a problem.

The curtain was open, and I could see directly into a bedroom. A boy and a girl both walked in and instantly started kissing. My face grew red. They didn't see me, but I felt awkward about it for some reason. They looked like they were in love. The girl pulled away from him and he started tickling her right away. She looked like she was having the time of her life. I smiled at them and wondered what it would be like to have a boyfriend. I've never had one before. The boys from back home didn't seem too interested in me, nor I them. They were all about sports and partying. I was more of a loner, besides Terra of course. I missed her so much already.

I walked away from the window and looked around the room. I'm glad I didn't have too much stuff. It wasn't going to take long for me to unpack and arrange everything how I wanted it to be. I walked over to the first box and opened it up. It was full of composition books that I wrote my poetry in. I opened one up and was about to begin reading a poem when I heard my mom's voice in the doorway.

"So, you found your room." She stated the obvious. I nodded my head. "How do you like it?" she asked as she walked in and looked around.

"It's okay." I said as I shrugged my shoulders. I liked the room, but I didn't want her to know that.

"What do you say you take a break from unpacking, and we go get some pizza for dinner? Maybe even stop off and check out Willows while we're there." She suggested with a half-smile. She stared at me like she was trying to study me.

"Are you asking, or do I have a choice?" I asked with an attitude.

"Well, if you are going to be snobby about it then I guess this isn't a request it is a demand." She crossed her arms. I rolled my eyes at her. "We leave in ten minutes; you better be in the car ready to go." She demanded before walking out of my room.

Ugh! I didn't want to go. I wanted to stay here and unpack. My mom was always unfair to me. I swear she hated me. We had nothing in common. She was the captain of the cheerleading squad when she was in high school, and I was the school weirdo. She didn't understand why I didn't play sports or try out for cheerleading. She apparently didn't know me very well. At least my dad tried to get to know me. He has tried a lot more than she has. She hated me and sometimes I hated her.

Chapter Three

Krystian

"Krystian!" I heard a familiar voice call my name. I turned around to see Rocco Orsburn walking up to me. He was wearing his yellow and white varsity athlete jacket with a plain white T-shirt underneath, along with his usual tight jeans that he still managed to sag in. He grabbed my hand and pulled me in for a hug and patted me on the back two times. He was strong. I thought he was going to rip my arm off. "Where have you been, bro? We hardly see you outside of school anymore." He towered over me by at least 5 inches. I was only 5'9.

"You know how my mom has been after Kameron." I tried to explain. "I had to sneak out just to be here tonight." I confessed.

"I heard about the divorce," his voice changed from happy to sad. "I'm sorry to hear that, bro. I know that must have been hard for you and your mom."

"Yeah man, it's been a real struggle, but it happens."

"Keep your head up, bro." He pulled me in for another hug. "I got to go find Tyrell really quick. I'll see you later."

"For sure." I told him.

"Don't be a stranger now, Krystian." He said to me as he walked off in a hurry to find Tyrell.

Rocco and Tyrell were both quarterbacks for our high school football team. They were both real good friends with Kameron. He was also on the football team and popular. He was the one who came to these parties. I was only here to see Andrea. Things were tough in our relationship because I couldn't do as much stuff as I used to. We used to be able to go on double dates with our friends, hang out at the local diner, sneak off and be alone. This past year has been a real drag. Losing my brother, my dad leaving my mom, not being able to see my girlfriend when I wanted to, and to make things worse, my grades have been dropping and my mom isn't pleased with me. She tried to have a talk with my dad about it, but he wasn't trying to hear it. Now he claims she is just nagging her all the time. My dad can be a real jerk to my mom sometimes. It's weird seeing them bickering back and forth like they can't stand each other when a year ago, we were like the perfect family. We are far from perfect now. We're not even a family anymore.

I walked through the crowded house of a fellow classmate, still searching for Andrea.

"Where could she be?" I asked myself out loud. I was stopped several times by other classmates saying "hey". They all looked surprised that I showed up. Who could blame them? This was more Kameron's scene, not mine.

"Well, I'll be damned," I heard a familiar voice say. "Look what the cat dragged in." I turned to see Debbie Garrison standing behind me. She hadn't changed a bit. Which I hadn't expected her to. It has only been a year since I had spoken to her. Debbie stood there with a big smile on her face. She wore her usual long black skirt and white blouse like she was going to Sunday services. Debbie was Kameron's girlfriend at the time of his death. They dated for about a year before the incident. I see her around school often, but we haven't spoken a word to each other since Kameron's funeral. Maybe a smile or two while passing in the halls. Mom always thought she was perfect for Kameron, but I think that was because she looked innocent in her long skirts and blouses, she wore every day. Debbie had my mom fooled big time. She was a party girl for sure. That's what attracted Kameron to her to begin with. My dad knew she wasn't innocent, but he still allowed them to date. Even without our parents' approval he still would have been with Debbie. He was infatuated with her. I was never sure why.

"Hey Debbie," I gave her a hug. She squeezed me tight. "How have you been?"

"Oh, I've had better days." She was slurring her words a little. "What brings you to this party? This was never your scene."

"I'm actually looking for Andrea. Have you seen her?"

"Have I?" she chuckled. "Yeah, she's around here somewhere."

I didn't know what she meant by that, but it made me curious. "Is she drunk?"

"You can do better than her and that's all I'm saying." She stumbled off before I could say anything else to her.

I started to grow angry thinking about what mess Andrea might have gotten herself into. Was she cheating on me? Was she arguing with someone? It wasn't like her to do anything wrong. She was a good person with a heart of gold. Was Debbie just too intoxicated and maybe saw something or heard something that wasn't what it seemed at all? I trusted Andrea one hundred percent. Why would I think she was doing anything like that? She loves me and wouldn't hurt me like that. I needed to find her and talk to her. I knew her well enough to know she would laugh at what Debbie said to me.

I searched the whole first floor of the house. I debated whether I should go upstairs and check first before going outside. Maybe she was up there with another guy. Stop, Krystian. Andrea isn't that kind of girl. She isn't cheating on you. I walked away from the staircase that led to the second floor of the house and went through the double glass doors in the kitchen. There were several people walking around outside, but it wasn't crowded. She wasn't outside either. If she was, she was hiding somewhere. I turned to walk back inside thinking to myself, maybe Andrea *was* cheating on me. I started to feel numb. If she was, I didn't want to know. I don't think I could handle that right now. I had to get out of here.

As soon as I walked back into the house, there she was standing in front of me.

"Krystian!" She jumped into my arms like she was happy to see me. "I'm so glad you're here."

"I have been looking all over the place for you." I was relieved to see her.

"I heard someone say that you were here, so I've been looking for you too." She responded then kissed me on the lips. Her breath smelt like alcohol, but I didn't mind it. I was just happy she was in my arms and not somebody else's. "I can't believe you snuck out of the house."

"I wanted to see you." I smiled at her. She returned the smile. "Can we take a walk?"

"Do you want to walk me home?" she asked. "This party is a drag anyways and I'm ready to go."

"Sure," I told her.

As we made our way to the front door, Tyrell and Rocco stopped us. Tyrell's brunet hair was a mess, like he just got into a scuffle.

"Had fun tonight, Andrea?" Tyrell smiled at Andrea. She smiled back at him. "Leaving so soon?"

"Sorry fellas, my boyfriend is here now. You can find entertainment elsewhere." She told them. I could feel my face getting hot. I was upset about the conversation they were having, and I didn't know why. How was she entertaining them? What was she doing with them? Was Rocco the one who told her I was looking for her? Did he know where she was the whole time? With Tyrell?

"Oh, come on, you are the best teammate ever."

"Hey Rocco, I thought you said you didn't know where she was?" I interrupted them. They all looked at me at the same time.

"Did I?" he smirked. "I was thinking of someone else."

"Why would I be looking for someone else?" I asked in a tone I wasn't used to talking in.

"No need for an attitude, Krystian. We were just playing some poker." Tyrell jumped in.

"Can we please go now?" Andrea pulled my arm towards her.

"Yeah, we can go now." I told her while staring at Rocco and Tyrell. They both had smirks on their faces like they were up to no good. Probably up to no good with my girlfriend.

I was silent as I walked Andrea home. She kept talking about the cheerleading squad and how she was looking forward to the next games. I wasn't interested in her cheer squad. I wanted to know why she was hanging around Tyrell and Rocco of all people. I always saw them as a bad influence when they hung out with Kameron.

"Why couldn't I find you at the party?" I blurted out. I just couldn't keep it in anymore.

"What are you talking about?" she asked, confused.

"I couldn't find you and I looked everywhere for you."

"Are you trying to accuse me of something, Krystian?" she asked angrily.

"I just asked where you were." I repeated myself. "I just think it's funny how Rocco claims he thought I was talking about somebody else when you're the only reason why I would be there in the first place.

Andrea stopped walking and looked at me in disbelief. "I can't believe you!" She said to me. "I don't know why Rocco says half the things he does. He is an idiot. I was playing poker with a group of people upstairs and that's why you didn't find me right away."

"Okay, I'm sorry." I tried to apologize.

"What is going on with you, Krystian? Why would you think I would ever cheat on you?" she demanded to know.

"I never said you cheated on me." I reminded her.

"Really? Because that's exactly what it sounds like you're accusing me of." She folded her arms across her chest, and she looked at me with her eyebrows raised. I knew she was angry by the way her nostrils flared out and her lips were tightened. She always made that face when she was mad at me for something.

"Can we please stop arguing?" I begged her as I grabbed her by her waist and tempted to kiss her. Andrea pushed me away from her.

"I'm not kissing you!" She shouted. "Did you really think that was going to fix everything?"

"I was hoping so." I admitted.

"Ugh! I'll walk the rest of the way home by myself." She shouted.

"But it's dark out here."

"I'm not afraid of the dark, Krystian." She didn't look back as she stormed off. I didn't chase after her. She was only a couple houses down from her street anyways.

I walked the couple of blocks home thinking Andrea would never cheat on me. She's not that kind of girl. She has never lied to me before so why would I think she was now? I am such an idiot. I have this great girl in my life and here I am trying to ruin it over nothing. My own thoughts were deceiving me. I love Andrea and I know that she loves me.

Chapter Four

Kora

Monday finally arrived and I dreaded my first day at my new school. My dad pulled up to a big one-story building. Willow Creek High School was plastered on the front of the building. Teenagers were scattered everywhere.

"Would you like me to come in with you?" he asked.

I looked at him, horrified. "No!" I told him. "Do you want them to make fun of me, Dad?"

"I'm sorry I even asked," he apologized. "I hope this school is a better fit for you than your last school, sweetie."

I looked at him and forced a smile on my face before climbing out of the vehicle. I knew he meant what he said, but I also knew changing schools wasn't going to change who I really am. I just hope someone at this place would like me for me. I hated pretending.

My first hour was Algebra. Algebra was my enemy. As much as I tried to understand it, the more confused I got about it. Why must I be tortured first thing in the morning? I might like Algebra during the end of the school day, but that much thinking as soon as I got here was too much for me to handle. I climbed into an empty seat and tried to be invisible. I was still nervous, being the new girl and all. A couple of students looked at me wondering who I was but none of them spoke to me.

"Mr. Lopez!" Mr. Thomas said in his deep voice. "Nice of you to finally join us."

"Better late than never." Said the cute guy that just disrupted the class by arriving late.

"You are right about that, Krystian. Now take a seat so I can get class started." Mr. Thomas told him in a deep, stern voice. Krystian sat in the seat next to me, which made me even more nervous. He was super cute. He glanced over at me and smiled. I politely smiled back at him. He leaned towards me, and I immediately started to blush.

"You're my new neighbor, right?" he whispered. I looked at him again studying his face. He *was* the guy I had seen in the window with the girl. I instantly felt let down. He had a girlfriend already. Not that he was into me or anything. He was probably just trying to be nice.

"Yeah," I finally answered him.

"I'm Krystian," he reached his hand out to shake mine. I reached my hand to his.

"Kora." Our hands touched and I had never felt hands so soft. Especially from a guy.

"Welcome to Willow Creek. It's probably lame compared to where you came from." He chuckled.

THE NEIGHBOR

"You know where I'm from?" I asked confused. How does he know anything about me if we had only just met?

"Your parents bought Willows?" he asked. I nodded my head without saying a word. "The town talks. Everyone is glad to see Willows isn't closing. It's the only good thing we got here in this hell hole. Are they going to change the name of it?"

"Mr. Lopez. Ms. Evans." Mr. Thomas interrupted our conversation before I could answer his questions. "Need I remind you that I am the only one that is supposed to be talking?" his eyebrows narrowed, and I knew instantly he was not playing around.

My face turned red with embarrassment. I felt the whole class staring at us. "I'm sorry." I mumbled as I put my head down.

"Sorry Mr. Thomas." Krystian said without hesitation. He must get in trouble a lot for talking, I figured. He looked like it didn't faze him at all.

"Now if you two are done, I would like to get back to teaching my class." He said.

Neither of us responded. Mr. Thomas waited a few seconds before continuing what he was trying to explain to the class.

The bell finally rang, and I gathered my book and placed it in my book bag. I couldn't wait to leave this classroom.

"Ms. Evans," Mr. Thomas called my name. "Can I please speak to you before you leave?"

I nodded my head yes and walked to his desk that was in front of the classroom. He waited until all the students were gone before speaking to me.

"Welcome to Willow Creek," he said as he gave a warm smile. "If I embarrassed you earlier, I apologize. You are new here and I can't tell you who you can and can't hang out with, but I'd be careful around Krystian Lopez."

"What do you mean?" I asked, confused. He seemed like a good person.

"Some might say he is a little damaged." Mr. Thomas replied.

"Aren't we all a little damaged?" I looked at him straight in the eyes without blinking. He started to look nervous. "Are you okay, Mr. Thomas?"

"I'm fine Ms. Evans," he cleared his throat. "You are free to go."

"You have a good day, Mr. Thomas." I smiled and left his classroom. Krystian was waiting for me in the hall.

"What did he say to you?" he asked curiously.

"Just welcome to the town and that I should stay away from you because you are damaged." I told him.

"What?" He stopped walking. "What does he mean by that?" he sounded upset.

"I don't know." I shrugged my shoulders. "I'm new here and I don't know anyone." I reminded him.

"I should go give him a piece of my mind. Who does he think he is?" he was looking at Mr. Thomas who was standing outside of his classroom greeting his next class.

"Go ahead." I dared him. He just looked at me and smirked.

"And here I thought you were some sweet and innocent girl."

I chuckled. "Not nearly." I admitted flirtatiously. He smirked. I almost felt guilty for flirting with him knowing I had just seen him days ago kissing a girl in his room. "I got to get to class. I'll talk to you later?"

"Sure thing. We are neighbors now." He pointed out.

I blushed as he walked away. I wanted to get to know him. He seemed like a cool person, and he was the first person to talk to me.

My first day of school went smoothly. I ran upstairs to my room and threw my bookbag on my bed. I looked out my window to see if Krystian had made it home yet. His curtain was open, but I did not see him in his room. I laid down on my bed and pulled my journal out of my bookbag. I started writing about how nice Krystian has been to me, how attracted I was to him, and how I hoped we could one day be together.

Chapter Five

Krystian

Andrea wanted me to come watch her at cheer practice. Usually, I'd tell her it was lame or make an excuse of why I couldn't go, but this time I owed her after what I accused her of doing. I still felt like a jerk. If you asked her, that's exactly how I should feel.

So here I was, sitting outside on the bleachers, watching the cheerleader's practice. I wasn't alone. The football team was on the field practicing along with the track team running laps. I couldn't help but think of a time when I used to sit out here and watch Kameron practice. Before he died, he was a junior and a quarterback for the team. He worked out a lot. I never saw the point. I guess sports just didn't interest me like they did him. A memory made its way to my mind.

Kameron had just finished practice. The coach was grilling the team for how poorly they practiced. Kameron ran up to me sitting in the stands.

"Hey little brother," he said out of breath. "You almost ready to go?"

"Yeah, Andrea is waiting for me." I told him frustrated. "Practice was supposed to end an hour ago." I complained to him.

"What happened to bros over hoes?" he chuckled. I didn't find the humor in his joke. When he noticed I wasn't laughing he immediately stopped. "Look, I'm sorry. I shouldn't have said that about Andrea. She is a good girl and nowhere near a hoe."

"I just want to get out of here." I demanded.

"Let me hit the showers really quick, okay?"

"Really Kameron?" I replied upset.

"I promise it won't take me more than twenty minutes." He ran off before I could even protest.

Forty minutes later, Kameron came out of the locker room looking clean. He wore his usual baggy jeans and a plain white T-shirt. A gold chain hung around his neck. Debbie had got him that necklace for their anniversary. It was something he cherished.

"You ready now?" he said looking happy.

"I've been ready, Kameron." I didn't hold back with how mad I was.

"Chill Krystian, it takes time to look this good." He smirked.

"Whatever, can we go now?" I was hoping he would say yes. I was hot and irritated, so I stood up Andrea. I would have never been at this practice if it hadn't been for Kameron getting in trouble for staying out past curfew and somehow, I got punished along with him.

I didn't talk to Kameron on the walk home because I was still upset with him, but he heard something.

"Krystian. Stop!" He exclaimed.

"What?" I asked with anger still in my voice.

"Do you hear that?" he was listening to his surroundings.

"What are you talking about?" I didn't hear anything. "Can we please go? You've already wasted my time today."

"You can't hear that?" he asked seriously. I tried to listen again to amuse him. This time I heard what he was hearing. It sounded like someone crying and two other voices that sounded familiar, but I couldn't place the voices.

"Where is it coming from?" I asked Krystian. He didn't respond right away.

"Behind Willows?" he didn't seem sure of himself. We both heard a cry for help and ran behind Willows to see who needed saving.

Kameron and I were both surprised to see Tyrell and Rocco in the alley behind Willows. On the ground next to the dumpster was Samuel Hernandez. He was crying and his nose was bleeding. Kameron looked at his teammates in shock.

"What the hell is going on here?" he asked them.

"Samuel fell and we were helping him up." Rocco lied.

"That's not what it looks like to me." I blurted out. Both Tyrell and Rocco gave me an evil look. The ones they give everybody they bully to warn them they will be next if they don't shut their mouth.

"Stay out of this, Krystian." Kameron demanded.

"Kameron, calm down. It's not what it looks like." Tyrell tried to convince him. We weren't stupid. We knew exactly what was going on.

"Samuel, are you okay?" Kameron asked him.

"He's fine." Rocco answered him instead.

"I didn't ask you, Rocco!" Kameron snapped.

"Why don't you mind your business?" Tyrell walked up to Kameron and now they were face to face. I felt anger building up in me and I was ready to explode. If any of these jerks touched my brother, I was going to snap. They were the biggest bullies in the school, and they managed to get away with everything they did wrong because they were on the football team, and they were the best players on the team along with Kameron. I didn't care how good they were. They had no right to bully anyone, especially Samuel. He was a kid with autism that always minded his own business. He never started trouble with anyone. They had no reason to be behind Willows hurting him.

"How about you get out of my face before you get hurt." Kameron said calmly back to Tyrell.

"Hey guys," Rocco tried to get in between them. "We are all friends here. Let's not do anything stupid."

"Looks like you already did that." I pointed out.

"Krystian, shut up!" Kameron shouted out to me without even looking at me. Why did he get to stand up to these guys and talk crap? Just because he knew them? Does he think I can't defend myself or something?

"Listen to your brother if you know what's best for you." Tyrell threatened me and Rocco chuckled. I didn't think it was funny and neither did Kameron.

"Let's get one thing straight," Kameron's tone turned into a one I've never heard him use before. His voice went deep and intimidating. It gave me chills down my spine. "You don't talk to my brother that way and we are no longer friends."

"Before you make a decision like that," Tyrell's smirk faded. "Maybe you should hear what he did to deserve this."

"I don't care what he did." Kameron didn't fall for it. "Krystian, help Samuel up. We are taking him home." Kameron's eyes were locked with Tyrell's. "And I will be letting the coach know what happened today."

I did what I was told and helped Samuel off the ground. His gray zip up hoodie had blood on it from his busted nose. His black curly hair that was overdue for a haircut was a mess. Samuel stood taller and bigger than me. If he knew how to defend himself, I knew he would be no match for Tyrell or Rocco.

THE NEIGHBOR

"We may even have the police called." Kameron threatened.

Rocco's eyes filled with fear and panic. "Kameron, don't do that." He begged. "We have a big game tomorrow; you know this game decides our future. I can't go to jail or have any kind of record."

"Should have made better choices then." Kameron showed no remorse.

"He's bluffing, Rocco." Tyrell called Kameron's bluff. "You know my dad is sheriff and he isn't going to do anything about it."

"Keep believing that." Kameron told him. "Let's go, Krystian."

We walked away from the alley and left Tyrell and Rocco standing there by themselves. In that moment I was proud of my brother. He stood up for Samuel and I never thought he would. I always labeled him as a jock bully just like Tyrell and Rocco. Today he proved me wrong. Unfortunately, Kameron and Samuel both died a couple nights after that. I pointed the blame on Tyrell and Rocco when it first happened, but they were questioned, and both had an alibi for the night of the murders. That's when the town started guessing and concluded that it had to be someone passing through. Kameron and Samuel were both beaten to death, so it had to be someone very strong to have had to take my brother on and beat him.

"So, what do you think of our new routines?" Andrea came out of nowhere and startled me. "Are you okay?" she asked.

"I'm fine." I lied. I felt this sadness come over me thinking about Kameron. I couldn't even fathom trying to explain it to Andrea. "They are good."

"Were you even paying attention, Krystian?" she crossed her arms and cut me with her eyes. "You barely even looked at me."

"What are you talking about?" I begged to differ. "I've been sitting here for an hour waiting on you."

"My point, Krystian!" She snapped. "Waiting on me. Not watching me!"

I was in no mood to deal with Andrea's crap today. The closer the date came to Kameron's death the angrier and sadder I grew. I didn't need her drama as well. She should know I needed space right now. Me coming here today meant something.

"Look, Andrea," I started to say.

"No! You look." Andrea put her hands on her hips and took a step towards me. We were now face to face like we were about to have a standoff. "You are going to pay attention to me, Krystian. You want us to break up because of your lack of attention?"

"No, I don't want to break up. Andrea, I love you." I cried out. Her just saying those words made my heart break instantly. She has never threatened me like that before.

"Then get it together, Krystian." She said in a stern voice and just turned around and walked towards a couple of other cheerleaders that were standing ten feet away, listening to us argue. They both rolled their eyes at me before they all walked off together. I was so pissed off that Andrea just walked away from me knowing I waited for her so we could spend time together. It's like I barely knew her anymore and I hated that fact because I loved her so much.

Chapter Six

Kora

I laid in my bed, thinking about Terra and how much I missed her. I knew she would love to hear about my new school and my new neighbor. Terra would listen to me for hours just venting and she would never judge me for anything. Always had advice attached to every response she gave. She was so smart and pretty. I remembered how we used to hang out together all the time. Terra was my only friend. She was the only person who really understood me. I hesitated to call her. I knew she wouldn't answer anyways. She wouldn't be answering any calls for a long time. Not after the accident that she had.

We were walking home from school one day discussing what we were going to do for the weekend. Terra wanted to go check out the county fair and I wanted to check out this new place that just opened called 'Let It Out'. They were having an open mic night and I always wanted to go to one. I couldn't ever imagine standing in front of a lot of people reading my material, but I found a sense of peace listening to other people express themselves in that form. Expressing themselves through raw material from their souls. It always did something for me. When I was younger, I would sit my dolls and stuffed animals in front of me and pretend they were my audience. I was still bashful while reading my work in front of them. Of course, they never judged me. My poetry is more developed now than it used to be. More mature and real. Life has really given me something to write about. I could never express myself out loud. At least not with anybody watching me.

"How about we go to the county fair during the day and then to open mic that night?" Terra suggested.

"Sounds like a plan to me." I agreed.

"I just have to let my mom know our plans in advance," she started to say. "You know how she can get with not knowing where I am at all times."

"Yeah, I know." I responded. "I'm glad my parents aren't like that." I knew exactly what she was talking about. Terra had a very strict mom. Her dad was in the Marines and while he was deployed overseas, her mom had to work two jobs just to support Terra and her little brother, Sonny. Sonny had to tag along with us several times because her mom had to work.

"Sonny will be with us at the fair, but not for open mic." She assured me.

"We are going to have so much fun." I said, not holding my excitement in. "I can't wait."

"Neither can…" Terra and I were both distracted by tires squealing behind us.

"Where do you weirdo's think you're going?" yelled Tommy Medina from the passenger seat of a blue Ford F150 that belonged to Marco Reyes. Tommy was the quarterback on the football team and, might I add, the popular boy in school. All the girls wanted to date him, and all the guys wanted to be him or the next best thing, his friend. It was pathetic really. Terra had a major crush on him as well, but I just couldn't see what the fuss was all about. Short brown hair, basic brown eyes. He wasn't even cute. He acted like almost every other quarterback at every other school. Just a bully who could get anyone to do anything just to add some sort of entertainment to his dull life.

Along with him were Marco and Steve Ortiz, who both played football with Tommy. Both were popular only because of him. Everywhere he went his entourage followed closely behind. They got their laughs by being bullies to the less popular group of kids. And I couldn't forget Carmella Vigil and Lizzy Brown, who were both sitting in the back seat of the truck. Carmella was the girl every guy wanted to date, and she thought she scored big when Tommy decided to make her his girl. She became Tommy in heels and lipstick. Lizzy was like her lap dog. Did everything for her and what she wanted. Lizzy wasn't mean to anyone. She was a good person that just hung out with the wrong crowd to get popularity points.

Terra and I both stopped walking as Tommy jumped out of the truck with a smirk on his face. We didn't have to say anything to each other because we already knew what he was about to do: terrorize the hell out of us. Steve jumped out of the back of the truck to join his friend. Marco placed his truck in the parked position but left it running. He then opened the door for Carmella and Lizzy to get out of the back seat. I grabbed Terra's arm and tried to turn around and walk the other way, pulling her to come with me, but Tommy jumped in front of us, and Steve stood behind us to make sure we weren't going anywhere.

"Where do you think you're going?" Tommy asked with a smirk still plastered on his face.

"Leave us alone!" I demanded. He just laughed and Steve did the same. I rolled my eyes at them. I looked at Terra who was shaking. I had to think of something to get them to leave us alone. Before I realized it, they were all standing around us.

"Why are we wasting our time on these creatures?" Carmella asked Tommy as she looked at me and Terra up and down with a disgusted look on her face.

Marco started laughing like what she said was funny. "She said creatures." He repeated. He was such a loser.

"That's what they are." Tommy got close enough to Terra to where they were now standing face to face. I glanced at Terra and knew she was terrified. Her body was trembling, and she looked Tommy in the eyes like she was a deer staring into head lights. I had to do something.

"Get away from her!" I pushed him back, but it didn't faze him at all.

"You going to let her talk to you like that, Tommy?" Steve taunted.

"Hell no!" He replied as he gave me a stare that made chills go down my spine. I didn't know what he was going to do to us, but I knew it was going to hurt. Tommy pushed me back and I fell hard on to the ground. I heard everyone laugh except Terra and Lizzy.

"Tommy!" Lizzy shouted. "What are you doing?"

"Carmella, shut your friend up!" He demanded. Tommy was back in Terra's face and yelling at her. I felt so hopeless.

"Do you want to end up like your friend?" he threatened. Terra shook her head no. "Then bark like a dog." He told her. Everyone started laughing again.

"What is your damage, Tommy?" Lizzy looked at him like she was disgusted with him.

"Last time Carmella, shut her up!" he yelled at his girlfriend.

"If you don't shut up, you can't hang out with us anymore." Carmella told Lizzy. Lizzy didn't respond. Instead, just brushed her blonde hair behind her ears and stood there watching nervously as she crossed her arms. I rolled my eyes at her for being so weak and controlled by these losers.

"Don't do anything he says, Terra." I shouted to her as I tried to climb off the ground but was immediately pushed back down by Marco. His foot was pressed hard into my stomach to try to keep me down. I cried out in pain but neither of them cared.

"The more you move the more it's going to hurt." Marco said to me with an ugly smirk on his face. I contemplated whether I should just give up or continue to get away from him.

"Bark like a dog or you end up on the ground like you friend here!" Tommy repeated himself. I could hear Terra start to cry. I wish I had the strength to hurt them all.

"Woof." Terra said softly. Everyone started laughing at her except Lizzy and Tommy.

"You call that a bark?" Tommy was not satisfied. "Do it again but this time louder."

"Record it this time, Tommy." Carmella suggested.

"Good idea, babe." Tommy replied. "Steve, go get your phone."

"Yes! This is going to be great." Steve said before running to the truck to get his phone.

"We can send it to the whole school." Marco suggested.

"Terra." I whispered her name. Terra looked back and down at me slowly. Her eyes were filled with tears. My heart crushed knowing my friend was in pain and embarrassed and I was stuck on the ground unable to help her. I laid my head down on the ground, feeling worthless. That's when I noticed it was a pencil on the sidewalk. When Tommy pushed me down, everything I had in my hands fell too and I always kept a pencil in my journal. I slowly reached for the pencil while everyone was distracted waiting for Steve to hurry up and grab his phone. I held it in my hand tightly.

"Here, I have it ready to go for you." Steve told Tommy.

"Make sure you get her face." Tommy instructed. "This is going to be awesome."

"It's recording now." Steve announced. I saw that as my opportunity to do something before they could hurt Terra anymore. All eyes were on Tommy, and I stabbed the pencil into Marco's leg as hard as I could then I jerked it downward until the wood broke in his leg. Marco screamed out and everyone came to his side.

"What happened?" Carmella cried out when she saw the blood starting to seep through his jeans.

Marco released me, not realizing he did so, and I jumped up and grabbed Terra's arm and started to run before anyone noticed.

"She stabbed me." Marco finally blurted out.

"Where did they go?" I heard Tommy yell.

"I didn't see them leave." Lizzy answered them.

"FIND THEM NOW!" Tommy screamed. "They can't be that far."

Terra and I hid behind a dumpster in the alley.

"They are going to find us." Terra cried. I knew she was terrified just as I was.

"Shush. No they won't." I assured her.

"Why did you do that?" she asked, trying to hold her tears back.

"I had to stop them somehow." I admitted.

"When they find us, they are going to kill us."

"Shush, someone is coming." I whispered to her. We both held our breath, scared it was Tommy. Terra was right, Tommy would kill us. Like *literally* kill us. He had no morals and never felt guilty for hurting anyone. The things he had done and got away with were unspeakable. Terra gripped my arm tightly. I knew she was scared, so was I. A face appeared in front of us, and we both let out a sigh. It wasn't Tommy, it was Lizzy. We both knew we weren't out of the woods yet. We did know Lizzy wasn't demented like Tommy, but she did hang out with them every day. She stood there and stared at us without saying a word. Her expression blank so she was hard to read.

"Did you find them?" Carmella's voice yelled out. That was the moment my life flashed before my eyes, not knowing if Lizzy was going to snitch on us or help us.

"Please, Lizzy." I whispered to her with tears falling down my face. Maybe she would have sympathy for us.

"No, they're not here." She yelled back to Carmella. She looked at me and Terra and whispered "Go now!" Then ran off.

"Tommy wants us to go around the whole block. The guys are on the other side of the block right now." We heard Carmella say to Lizzy. We waited a couple of seconds until we couldn't hear them talking anymore.

"Let's go." I told Terra and stood up.

"What if they find us?" she was still crying.

"They won't if we hurry up." I tried to convince her. We slowly walked out of the alley, both constantly looking behind us and listening for them. We came to the street, and I noticed Marco's truck was still running.

"What a moron." I said out loud.

"What are you doing?" Terra asked, scared. She knew exactly what I was about to do. "Kora don't do it. We will be in a lot of trouble."

"We won't go far, okay? Just away from these psychos and we'll leave the car on the side of the road." I convinced her. It sounded like a good idea at the time, and it would have been if we hadn't been caught.

"Kora!" My mom's voice came out of nowhere and I realized where I was again. I wiped a single tear from my eye without her noticing. That whole incident with Tommy is the reason why we had to move away from our lives in Phoenix. I hated him for what he did to me, and especially for what he did to Terra.

"What is it, Mom?" I asked her softly.

"Your dad and I are going out to dinner," she said. "Would you like to go with us?"

THE NEIGHBOR

"Sure Mom," I said even though I wasn't in the mood to hang out with my parents, but I knew I wanted to get along with my mom so she could start to trust me again. I missed the bond that we used to have before Tommy ruined my life. "Will you give me ten minutes to get ready?" I asked her.

"Sure," she smiled at me. "We'll be downstairs waiting for you." She walked out of my doorway, and I could hear the stairs creak as she descended. I closed my journal and climbed out of bed to get ready.

Chapter Seven

Krystian

"So, who do you think did it?" Mom asked, catching me off guard as I ate breakfast.

"What are you talking about? I asked.

"You know what I'm talking about." She raised her left eyebrow, and I knew instantly what she meant.

"Do you think we should be having this conversation right now?" I didn't want her to be sad talking about Kameron.

"Look Krystian, I have an apology to make to you." She sat down in the seat across from me.

"What are you talking about?" She didn't owe me anything.

"This past year I have been so caught up in losing Kameron and then the divorce, I forgot I had another son. The way I have treated you was not fair to you at all."

"Mom, no need to apologize." I told her. "I understand. I knew you just needed time. You were never a bad mom and I'm sorry again for what I said to you the other day."

"That's part of why I wanted to talk to you."

"What do you mean?" I was confused. I placed my spoon back into my bowl and gave her my full attention.

"I'm always going to worry about you because you are my son, but I know I need to unhook the leash. I want you to have a normal life and be able to hang out with your friends when you want to, and I know you can't do that with me being constantly paranoid." She explained.

"Mom, it's okay." I tried to convince her.

"That's just it, Krystian," she grabbed my hand and held it. "I need to get out of this funk I've been in, and I know I have been slacking as a mother with all the extra hours I've been picking up at work and what I'm trying to say is that I'm sorry. I'm done feeling sorry for myself and I'm ready to find justice for your brother."

"What do you mean find justice?" I didn't understand where she was coming from. No one knew what happened to Kameron and Samuel that night. At least that's what everyone has been saying.

"I talked to the detective a couple of days ago and he has some questions about Kameron's case, and he wanted to talk to you about it."

"What questions, Mom? I've told the police everything I knew about that day." I pulled my hand away from hers and stood up, feeling confused and angry. "Why after almost a year do they want to start investigating? They should have found the guy that did this to Kameron when it happened."

"It's been a year and people will start to remember things they couldn't at the time it happened. Or somebody might start talking. They just want to see if anyone's story has changed from a year ago."

"And what if it's not?"

"Then it's not but I know in my heart that someone somewhere knows what happened to Kameron and Samuel that night and we will get answers, I promise you that." My mom sounded so sure of herself. I didn't know what to think. I told the detectives about what happened that day in the alley with Tyrell and Rocco but for some odd reason, the recording from the alley was gone so it was their word against mine. And who better to have your back than a sheriff as a dad? I'm almost positive his dad destroyed the evidence. Neither of them was suspects in the case, so it didn't matter what happened to the video or that Tyrell's dad was the town's Sheriff. All that mattered was they had two teenagers dead and no clues on who did it. The town always talked about a passerby. I can't say that's not who did it, but it left a lot of questions unanswered. Why would Kameron be with Samuel in the middle of the night unless he saw Tyrell and Rocco picking on him again? Why would Samuel be at the party anyway? He never got invited to any of them. I know there is more to the story. I just wish we knew what it was. I hate what happened to my parents' marriage and how it left me feeling alone.

"I get what you're saying Mom, and I want to find out whoever did this to Kameron as well." I told her. "I'll do what I have to do to help."

"Your dad will be here later today. We are going to ride together to go talk to a reporter."

"A reporter?" I asked.

"Yes, we want to get Kameron and Samuels story out. Someone somewhere knows something and if the police don't want to help us, then we must act ourselves."

"Do you want me to go too?" I offered, not really wanting to go, but I would.

"No, It's a nice day out. Take Andrea to the lake or something. The jet ski hasn't been used in a while and I know Andrea used to love riding it with you." She suggested. I was relieved that I didn't have to go with them. I wouldn't even know what to say to a reporter.

"How am I supposed to get to the lake, Mom?" Did she really think I would walk there? "I don't even have a car."

"I told you that your dad was riding with me." She answered.

"And?"

"You can drive his truck. You have a license, don't you?"

"Well yeah but will Dad let me?" I was in shock that she even suggested it.

"You let me handle your father and you just can start making plans with Andrea." She said with confidence. I wasn't going to argue with her. I knew she would be able to convince my dad to do anything. As much as they bickered back and forth, I knew deep down they still had love for each other.

"Thank you so much, Mom. I'm going to go call Andrea right now. I know she's going to be so happy to hang out." I kissed her cheek and hurried upstairs to my room to call Andrea.

I called Andrea three times, and she didn't answer. "She's probably still asleep." I said out loud to myself. Andrea was known for sleeping in on the weekends. I decided to send her a text message so she would see it first thing when she woke up.

Hey beautiful, I know you're probably still asleep, but I made plans for us today just you and me. I can't wait to tell you what it is. Call me as soon as you get up. I love you.

I hit send and threw my phone on my bed. I pulled open my dresser drawer and searched for some clothes to wear so I could shower.

It was already 2 p.m. and Andrea never responded to me. My dad was already here, and he and my mom were about to leave.

"We got to go pick up Samuel's parents as well so we could all ride together." My mom said to me before walking out the front door. My dad was right behind her but stopped and looked at me.

"I left some money on the table for you for gas and food. We are going to be gone for a while so make sure you eat and drive carefully. Tell Andrea we said hi. Love you, kiddo." He said before following my mom out the door. I locked the door behind them and tried to call Andrea again. This time it went straight to voicemail. Why isn't she answering me? She has never avoided me like this. I decided to just go to her house and check on her. She was probably sick or something, or maybe she had lost her phone.

I pulled up to Andrea's yellow house that was only a couple of blocks from mine. Her mom's car was parked in the driveway. I walked up to the white front door and knocked three times. Simon, Andrea's youngest brother, answered with his short brown hair sticking up all over the place like he had just woken up.

"Hey there Simon, where's Andrea at?" I asked nicely.

"She's not here." He responded in a sleepy voice.

"Are you sure?" I asked just in case. "Can you check to see if she's in her room, please?"

"Hold on!" He said rudely but walked away to check for me. He returned less than a minute later. "Like I said she's not home. Now go away!"

"Damn, okay!" I said rudely back. Simon slammed the door in my face. I reached for my phone out of my back pocket to dial Andrea's number. I hit the call button and it went straight to voicemail once again. I didn't know where Andrea was or why she wasn't answering my calls. She usually calls me every day when she wakes up and throughout the day. What is going on with her? I drove back home and wondered what else I could do. I didn't want the day to go to waste. As I pulled the truck into my driveway, I noticed Kora walking out of her house. She sat down on her porch with a notebook in hand. I had the perfect idea. I was about to get to know the girl next door.

Chapter Eight

Kora

I sat outside on the porch writing in my book. I was working on a poem but for some reason, writer's block had taken over my brain. I was starting to feel frustrated.

"Whatcha doing?" a familiar voice asked, startling me. I jumped, grabbing my chest. Krystian laughed.

"You scared me." I said, trying to catch my breath.

"Obviously." He continued to laugh.

"It's not funny." I threw my pen at him playfully, but he caught it instead.

"Yes, it was. You should have seen your face."

I rolled my eyes at him. "What do you want Krystian?" I finally asked.

"I'm bored," he admitted. "I wanted to ask if you wanted to go hang out at the lake with me?"

"Really?" I was surprised that he would even want to hang out with me.

"Yes, really. And I won't take no for an answer."

"Then why ask?" I said sarcastically.

"Ha! Good one, Kora." He faked a laugh. "Now go change so we can go." He pointed to the front door of my house.

"What makes you think I can even go?" I asked curiously.

"Because I know your parents aren't here. They are working at Willows tonight and we will be back way before they even close shop, so they won't even know that you left."

"You have it all figured out, don't you?" I teased.

"Pretty much," he had a devious smirk on his face. "I'm good like that."

I laughed at him. He had a cute personality. Charming. "I can't go to the lake." I frowned.

He looked disappointed. "Why not?"

"I don't have a swimsuit." I admitted, putting my head down with embarrassment.

He started laughing again. "That's not a problem. Do you have shorts?"

"No."

"Are you serious?"

"Yes, I'm serious." I said defensively.

"I got a pair you can wear. Now let's go." He demanded me again. I didn't respond. I just climbed up from the porch and threw my book in my bag and followed him next door to his place.

We had to drive over thirty minutes to get to the lake. Our small town didn't have one, but two towns over there was one. Krystian laughed at me when I ducked down in the passenger seat as we passed Willows. It looked busy but I wasn't about to let my parents see me. They finally let me stay home alone and I knew they would freak out and never let me do it again if I was caught. We pulled up to the lake in his gray F150. He brought along his jet ski. He backed into the lake, making sure the trailer was deep enough in the water.

The place looked deserted. Maybe about three families were here. Several little kids were splashing in the water while an older, overweight man cooked on the grill. Other adults sat at the table with him laughing together. I wondered what that was like. My family never laughed like that. We never went to social events. Maybe because I wasn't very social, and they were embarrassed by me. Or because of what I had done in the past.

"Can you help me with this?" I heard Krystian say. I hadn't even noticed he got out of the car. I climbed out and rushed to help him.

"What do you need me to do?" I asked, ready to help.

"Just help me untie this and we are going to push it into the lake." He explained. I did as I was directed. After getting the jet ski into the water he handed me a life jacket.

"Safety first." He said.

"What is this for?" I asked, confused.

"To put on. I can't let you ride without it."

"I don't want to ride." I admitted. I had never ridden on a jet ski. I had never swam a day in my life.

"It will be fun," he tried to convince me. "You will have the time of your life."

I was embarrassed to admit that I couldn't swim, but I knew I had to if I wanted to get out of riding this thing. "Krystian…" I began to say. I put my head down.

"Don't tell me you don't know how to swim." He already knew what I was going to say. He looked shocked. "You're a weird girl, Kora. You don't own shorts and you've never went swimming before. Have you been locked up your whole life?" He joked but I didn't take it as a joke. If only he knew the real me. I wanted to run off and cry. "I'm sorry if I upset you. I was just joking." He saw the sad look on my face and knew what I was thinking.

"I'll ride with you." I blurted out with regret. He already thought I was weird and if he finds out that I'm not fun either, he may never ask me to hang out with him again. I liked him more than I should, and I wanted to be in his world. And if that means doing stuff I would have never done before, then so be it.

"Are you sure?" he asked.

"Yep." I said quickly and grabbed the life jacket from him. He helped me put it on and I climbed on the back of the jet ski behind him.

"Put your arms around my waist so you don't fall off." He looked back at me.

"Okay." I said nervously. I wrapped my arms tight around him. I was terrified once he started the engine, and as we got going. He started out slow then gradually got faster. I finally opened my eyes once I wasn't scared anymore. It was amazing how much adrenaline I had. We were driving through the water. It was exciting. I had this rush I've never felt before. I finally was able to relax behind him. I heard myself laughing.

"Are you having fun?" he yelled back at me.

"This is great." I yelled over the wind. I was lost in a world I had never been to before. I had been missing out on life. Why didn't my parents ever do fun stuff like this with me? I had forgotten about all my troubles and was lost in this moment with Krystian.

"I told you." He bragged. "Hold on."

He turned a little and I found myself flipping off the jet ski and landing into the water. My head went under, and I went into a panic. I thought I was about to drown. I started swinging my arms and legs hoping I was doing it right. I floated to the surface, spitting water out of my mouth. Taking that breath meant everything to me. I had forgotten that I put a life jacket on. Otherwise, I may have already been dead. I looked around for Krystian, terrified I was going to go underwater again. I saw him turn around on the jet ski.

"KRYSTIAN!" I screamed out his name. He had just noticed that I wasn't behind him anymore. I tried to keep my head above water until he reached me. I paddled towards him. I don't know why, I couldn't swim. I was just relieved to see him. Krystian pulled up next to me and reached his hand to me.

"Grab my hand!" He yelled. He could tell I was in a panic. I grabbed his hand, and he pulled me up. "Are you okay?" he asked. I nodded my head as I continued to breathe slowly to stop my heart from racing. I was shocked he lifted me up like that with one hand. He was a lot stronger than I thought he was. "Hold on tight this time." He said before starting the engine.

"STOP!" I screamed. He stopped the engine with no hesitation.

"What's wrong?" He asked in a panic.

My face grew red and my body hot. I didn't want to tell him, but I had no choice but to. I covered my face with both my hands and whispered, "I have no shorts on."

What did you say?" he asked in confusion.

"I have no shorts on." I repeated myself louder with my hands still covering my face. I heard Krystian bust out in laughter. Which made me even more embarrassed. I began to cry. I have never been so embarrassed in my life.

"Don't cry," he begged me. "We'll find them." He looked around the lake and spotted them floating nearby. He jumped off the jet ski and swam to them. I watched him as he grabbed the shorts and swam back towards me. I wiped the tears from my eyes relieved that they were found. I couldn't imagine having to ride home without any shorts on. I didn't grab any extra clothes because I didn't plan on swimming or anything. I just wanted to sit by the water and write.

"Here," he handed me the shorts. "I saved them for you." He smiled.

I returned the smile. "Thank you." I told him. "Will you please turn around so I can put them on?"

He chuckled but did what was asked of him. I hurried and slid the shorts on and made sure the strings were tied tight. I wasn't going to risk losing them again. "Is it safe now?" Krystian asked.

"Yes." I said in a low voice. Krystian climbed onto the jet ski. It wobbled and I thought it was going to flip over again.

"I'm not going to let you fall again." He promised.

"Please don't." I said to him softly.

"Hold me tight and I'll take us back to the shore." He said. "I'll go slow this time."

The engine started once more, and I became scared once again. I held him super tight. I wasn't sure if he could breathe or not, but I didn't care. I wasn't going to fall off again. Thank goodness we weren't too far out, and he returned us to the shore within a minute. I never felt so safe as my feet touched the ground. A sigh of relief escaped my body. My legs began to feel like putty. I fell into the shallow water.

"Are you okay?" Krystian rushed to my side and sat me up.

"I don't know?" I was scared. "My legs just started to feel weak."

"Here I'll help you up." He wrapped his arms around my waist and pulled me up. We froze staring into each other's eyes. I wanted to kiss him so bad, but I knew I couldn't. He had a girlfriend, and I didn't know how he felt about me. I was the first to look away.

"I think I need to sit down for a minute." I blurted out.

"Of course," he looked around for something. "Lean up against the jet ski and I'll go find us something to sit on. I watched him carefully as he returned to the truck and searched his bag for something to sit on. As much as I have embarrassed myself today, I wouldn't trade this day for the world.

Chapter Nine

Krystian

I placed a towel on the ground so we could sit in what sun we had left to dry off with. Kora was still trying to catch her breath. I giggled still thinking about today's events. Never had I been in a situation like that before and I know how embarrassed she must have felt, but the more I thought about it the more hilarious it became.

"What are you giggling about?" she asked standing above me with water still dripping from her hair and body.

"Nothing." I lied to save her from turning even redder than she is now. "Sit," I ordered. She did what was instructed. I knew she was still embarrassed. Her breathing hadn't calmed down yet either. I could tell she was nervous; I was nervous too for some odd reason, but it made her that much cuter. She had a strand of wet hair stuck to her cheek. I gently grabbed it, but she flinched. I let go instantly not wanting to scare her. I knew something bad had to have happened to her for her to flinch when I barely touched her. I was even more curious about her.

"I'm just trying to move your hair out of your face." I assured her. She didn't respond so I reached up again and grabbed the wet strand of hair from her face and gently placed it behind her ear. I started to feel nervous and excited at the same time. She looked at me and I instantly wanted to know what she was thinking. Our eyes were locked once again. I realized my hand was behind her neck. Instead of moving my hand, I pulled Kora closer to me and I kissed her. My heart was beating so hard I thought it was going to pound right out of my chest. Why was I so nervous? I didn't want to stop kissing her. Kora's lips were soft, and they fit perfectly on mine. I was lost in the moment until I felt her push me away from her. I looked at her without saying anything. I thought she was enjoying it as much as I was.

"We can't," Kora mumbled answering the question I never asked. "Andrea."

I can't believe I had forgotten about Andrea. I didn't know what to say. "Oh," I finally said. "I'm sorry." I stuttered.

"It's okay." She said softly, now feeling embarrassed over something completely different. We sat there in awkward silence. I didn't know what to say to her. I wondered what she was thinking. Did she regret kissing me? I hoped not. I enjoyed every second of it. I didn't want to scare her away. Was I wrong for what I did? Even though I'm with Andrea kissing Kora didn't feel wrong to me. What does that mean? Everything became confusing to me all at once.

"The sun is setting." She broke silence and pointed out to the sky.

I looked at it and it looked perpetual. From the different shades of orange consuming the sky, the rosy clouds scattered throughout, the way the rays of the sun glared in waves across the water. I had never sat and watched the sunset before. It made me feel warm. It made me feel human. It was speechless. It was breathtaking. It was perfect. Just like today had been.

I looked over at Kora and she looked like she was staring at the most beautiful thing she had ever seen. She looked at peace. Like in this moment nothing was wrong. She was taking a break from hurting. I knew she was, because I was. I smiled for real today. I didn't have to fake it. Kora made me feel like a real person. I didn't have to fake laughter like I did with Andrea. I didn't have to walk on eggshells like with Andrea either. I love Andrea and with Kameron's memorial coming up you would think she would be here for me knowing that I am hurting, but instead I'm being ignored like I'm nothing. Had Andrea answered her phone and come with me today, I know for a fact it wouldn't have been memorable like today with Kora has been.

I heard a loud growling sound come from Kora's stomach. She wrapped her arms around her belly as if she was trying to hide the sound.

"Are you okay?" I asked her concerned.

"Yeah, I'm fine." She answered, embarrassed.

"You're hungry, aren't you?" I already knew what was wrong.

"I'll be alright." She lied.

"As much as I don't want this evening to end. I'm starving as well." I admitted. "I know this little pizza place in town we could try out."

"Sure," she said softly.

I helped Kora off the ground, and we headed to the truck. After putting the jet ski onto the trailer, we headed in town to Tom's Pizza Galleria.

I watched Kora stuff her mouth with a slice of peperoni pizza and wash it down with a Dr. Pepper. I felt bad for making her wait to eat this long. I guess I was so caught up in the moment I forgot we had to eat too. I noticed she had pizza sauce on her chin. I chuckled then grabbed a napkin to wipe it off her.

"What are you doing?" she flinched again.

"Relax, I was just going to wipe the sauce off your face." I told her.

"I can do it." She grabbed the napkin out of my hand and wiped her chin off herself.

"So, what's your story?" I finally asked.

"What do you mean?" she tilted her head to the side.

"Why are you here?" I asked a different way.

"Because this is where you brought me." She frowned.

I started to laugh. "No, I mean why did you move to Willow Creek?"

Kora was reluctant to answer the question. She seemed to have spaced out for a second.

"Hello? Kora?" I tried to get her attention.

"What is your story?" she asked like I didn't notice she just spaced out. Instead of pointing out that she just changed the subject to me instead of her, I went along with it.

"Well, where to start." I was hesitant, but I knew in order for her to open up, I had to open up too. "My parents are divorced."

"That sucks! Why did they split up?" she asked.

"Because of my brother." I know it wasn't Kameron's fault, but in a way it was.

"Your brother split them up?" she asked in disbelief.

"Yeah, it's his fault they divorced." I admitted. I wanted to play with her a little just to see how she would react.

"What did he do?" She was curious. Little did she know she wouldn't be expecting what I was about to tell her.

"He got murdered." I blurted out. Kora was taking a drink from her cup when I said that, and soda went all over me.

"I am so sorry." She said as her face got the reddest it had been all day. "I didn't mean to do that."

I was laughing so hard everybody looked at us. "It's okay I swear." I tried to convince her as she struggled to grab napkins to clean up the mess she had made. In the process she ended up knocking the cup over and the rest of the soda spilled over the rest of the pizza. She gave up and placed her head into her hands.

"Are you crying?" I asked.

"I can't believe I just did that." She said through her tears.

"It's okay." I assured her. She was delicate.

"No, I ruined your dinner." She removed her hands from her face and her eyes were red from crying. I felt bad for her. It wasn't a big deal to me, but I knew it was for her.

"Is everything okay?" the waiter asked, concerned.

"Yes, a drink got spilt but it's okay." I told her. She looked at Kora making sure what I said was the truth.

"Everything's fine." Kora said softly.

"Let me get you a refill." She smiled and grabbed Kora's cup off of the table. "Dr. Pepper, right?"

Kora nodded her head and the waiter walked off. I grabbed a slice of soggy pepperoni pizza and took a bite of it.

"What are you doing?" Kora asked frantically.

"I'm not wasting this." I confessed. "It's still good."

"You're nuts." Kora started laughing and it was the first time I heard her laugh all day.

We sat at the pizza joint for at least two hours. She told me about missing her friend Terra Silva and I told her about what happened to my brother. At least what we think had happened to my brother. It was a nice talk that I really needed to let out. And by the way she acted, she needed to talk about her friend and how much she missed her. I learned Kora was human just like everyone else. She held back on saying a lot of stuff to me, but I was going to get it out of her one way or another. I had to know everything I could about her and I knew we were going to have more days like today in our future.

Chapter Ten

Kora

"Thank you for today." I told Krystian as I climbed out of his truck.

"I hope you don't get into too much trouble seeing how it's nighttime already." He was concerned. I was flattered he was worried about me. We had lost track of time eating dinner. I looked at my house next door and saw the kitchen light on. I knew instantly I was in trouble. My parents were home. I looked back at Krystian who was still staring at me with a concerned look on his face. I smiled at him, and he smiled back.

"I'm sure I won't be in that much trouble." I lied to him. I couldn't tell him how extra my parents were, and they were probably already looking for a new home for us to move to. "I'll see you tomorrow?" I asked nervously, hoping he would say yes.

"Of course," he smiled and waved bye to me as I strolled home. My face was starting to hurt from the biggest smile I ever wore in my life. I had this feeling of Krystian.

I walked through my front door and both my mom and dad were standing there looking at me, disappointed. My smile disappeared within an instant. Maybe I could talk myself out of this one.

"Where have you been?" my mom demanded to know, her voice filled with anger. "Answer me now!"

"I went with Krystian to the lake." I answered honestly. There was no point in even trying to lie to them. That always got me nowhere. "Then we went out for pizza."

"How dumb do you think I look?" Mom didn't believe me. And I wanted to answer that question so badly, but I knew it would result with my death.

"I'm not lying, Mom!" I cried out. "Dad!" I looked at him hoping he would defend me or say something, but he didn't say anything. Just put his head down. I knew he was disappointed that I snuck out of the house, but I know he would have understood if it wasn't for my mom constantly controlling him.

"Even if what you are saying is true, who gave you permission to do that?" my mom folded her arms across her chest. Her eyes narrowed and I could see the vein ready to pop out of her forehead. She was angry. Very angry, and I didn't understand why. I thought hanging out with Krystian would make her happy. I made a friend and now I'm being punished for it.

"You two were gone and left me here alone like you always do. I'm not allowed to have a phone, so it's not like I could have asked you for permission." I argued.

"That is not a good enough excuse!" My mom argued back. "How were we to know who you were with and what you were doing?"

"Maybe allow me to have a phone." I said, hoping they would agree with me.

"You know why you are not allowed a phone." My mom said without even blinking an eye. I knew better than suggesting that.

"We were worried sick about you." My dad finally got the nerve to speak.

"Was you really worried about me or were you more worried about what I might have done to someone else?" I asked. They both looked at each other, both scared to answer the question. "That's what I thought!" I began to walk away. I was tired of being attacked over something I did that wasn't even my fault. Even though I'm the one who got blamed for everything.

"That's not fair to us." My mom stopped me. "You know exactly what you have put us through back home. Did you really think we could forgive you that easily?"

"I knew you would never forgive me for ruining your perfect life. I'm sorry you didn't have an abortion when you had the chance to." I yelled in her face and wished I could unsay what I just said. I thought I actually saw a tear forming in one of her eyes.

My mom slapped me hard across the face. "Helen!" My dad said in shock. I instantly put my hand over my face. I was in shock as well. My mom has never hit me before. My face stung from the slap, and I debated on whether or not I should hit her back. Oh, I really wanted to. Instead, I bumped her out of my way with my shoulder and ran upstairs to my room. I threw myself on my bed and cried. How could the best day of my life turn into a disaster like this? Why am I still being punished for something that wasn't my fault? I could hear my parents arguing about me downstairs. Now my dad wanted to defend me. "How could you hit her like that Helen!" My dad yelled at my mom.

"She deserved it!" She fired back with no remorse. "And you just let her talk to me the way she did!"

"We promised we weren't going to raise her like that." My dad argued.

"Haven't you noticed who she really is?" my mom scolded. "Don't you think she turned out this way because of our lack of discipline?" My mom was so sure of herself. I couldn't bear to listen to it anymore. I pulled out my journal and took all my anger and frustration out on my mother. I wrote about how much I hated her, and I wish she didn't exist. How could she treat me the way she does? Does she not like me? I don't even think she loves me. It just feels like she is out to destroy me because of one mistake that I had made. Why can't she not forgive me like my dad has? She has a grudge against me like I did something to her.

Chapter Eleven

Krystian

After getting home I tried to call Andrea again and she still wasn't answering the phone. At this point I was worried. It's not like her to not talk to me unless she was upset with me and even then, she had no problem letting me know how she felt.

After unloading the jet ski back into the garage, I went upstairs to my room. My mom wasn't back yet so that meant the interview took longer than expected. She hadn't called me either. I debated whether I should call her to make sure she was okay. I know it must have been hard for her to have to talk about Kameron. It was hard for me to think about him without my eyes getting watery. I dialed my mom's number and hit the call button. She answered after one ring.

"Hey dear, what are you doing?" she asked.

"I'm just calling to check on you." I told her.

"We are on our way back now. We decided to have dinner after the interview." she confessed.

"How did it go?" I was curious to know.

"It went well. How was your day with Andrea?" she asked cheerfully.

"I didn't go with Andrea." I admitted.

"Oh, so you just stayed home all day?" she asked in disbelief.

"No, I took Kora instead." I said casually.

"Kora? Who is Kora?" she sounded confused.

"The girl next door mom."

"Oh, well I hope you had a good evening. I will talk to you when I get home. Your dad is driving right now, and you know he is blind as a bat driving at night, so I have to be his second pair of eyes." She said.

"Okay mom, I love you and see you in a little bit." I replied.

"I love you too, Krystian. I'll see you in about an hour."

"Love you, son." I heard my dad's voice in the background.

"Love you too, Dad." I told him.

"Bye." My mom said softly.

"Bye mom." I said then hung up the phone.

I let out a sigh and sat up in my bed. My curtain was open and wondered about Kora. I had the most fun I have had in a really long time. Kora wasn't what I expected her to be. The way she dressed, the way she acted. She was a shy girl. Mysterious for sure and I wanted to be the one to crack the code on who she really was. When I first laid eyes on her I had to know her. At first it was just to be her friend, but after today, I want to be her everything. Being with Andrea has had its moments but we always chose each other in the end. Now there are so many thoughts going through my head. Why hasn't Andrea been answering my calls? Who is she with? Who has my time with Andrea? Those are questions I can't answer without talking to Andrea.

I glanced out my bedroom window into Kora's room. Her black curtains were open, and she was lying in bed. I noticed she was writing in her journal. I thought it was cute that a seventeen-year-old girl kept a journal. I wondered if she was writing about me. About how fun our day was, or that amazing kiss we had. All the embarrassing moments that made her ten times cuter than any other girl in Willow Creek.

Headlights caught my distraction. My mom and dad were home. I looked at Kora one last time before closing my curtain. I ran down the stairs to greet my parents.

"How did everything go?" I asked them both as soon as they walked in the door.

"I think we may have accomplished something." My mom said in a tired voice.

"At least we hope we did." Dad gave his opinion.

"So, what's the plan?" I asked anxiously.

"They are going to do a news broadcast on the anniversary of Kameron and Samuels death next week." Mom began to say.

"They are hoping someone sees it and remembers something suspicious that night or may come forward." Dad cut her off.

THE NEIGHBOR

"Do you think it will work?" I asked.

"It's better than sitting back and not doing anything." Mom said as she hung her purse on the coat rack.

"It's almost been a year, son, and we are trying to do everything we can to find out who did this and why." Dad added.

"Is there anything I could do to help?" I asked, ready to do anything I possibly could.

"As a matter of fact, you can." Mom said with raised eyebrows. I knew she was about to ask me something I didn't want to do.

"What is it?" I asked dreadfully.

"You can go shopping with me to find you something suitable to wear for the broadcast."

"You mean I have to be on TV?" I wasn't too happy with that idea.

"Why wouldn't you be?" my dad asked sternly. "You are a part of this family, aren't you?"

"Yeah but..."

"No but's about it. You will do this for your brother." Mom interrupted before I could finish what I was going to say.

"Don't you want justice for your brother?" Dad asked.

"Yes," I answered. "I just didn't know I'd have to be on television."

"It's a good thing, Krystian." Mom assured me. "We need the public's help in finding this person or persons. Don't be so selfish. We couldn't save your brother so let's at least try to find out who did this and why."

My mom was right. I had to stop being selfish and get back to reality. Kameron was dead and we still didn't know who, what, or why. "You are right, Mom," I told her, feeling ashamed. "I'm sorry "

"Don't beat yourself up, kid," Dad said. "You're just a teen and I know a lot of this doesn't make sense to you." He put his hand on top of my head and rubbed it, messing my hair up.

I chuckled. "Stop, Dad." Before I knew it, he had me in a head lock, rubbing my head harder. As I laughed, I tried to break free from him, but he was a lot stronger than I was.

"You two cut it out!" Mom ordered us.

"I have to toughen him up somehow." Dad joked.

"I am tough." I claimed.

"Not tough enough." Dad said laughing.

"Krystian, go get your dad a blanket and pillow out of the storage closet so I can set the couch up for him."

"You're staying?" I looked at my dad with excitement.

"Just for the night." He said.

"You know your dad can't see that well at night." Mom added.

THE NEIGHBOR

"Okay!" I said and did what I was told.

As mom made the couch up, my dad and I stood there watching her. She made sure the sheet was perfect and the pillow was placed just right.

"Geez Mom," I said wondering what the point of all that was. "He's just going to mess it all up when he lays on it."

"I don't mind at all son," Dad said. "You know your mom likes everything to look nice." Dad was right about that. I think my mom had OCD or something. Everything had to be in their place and facing the right way. Kameron and I used to get her so upset when we were younger by moving her knick-knacks around in the living room. Or by doing random stuff like switching the plates and cups in the cabinets. She would always yell for our dad to handle us so she could hurry up and fix what we had done. Dad couldn't keep up with us back then. He was a little on the hefty side. He had lost so much weight since I was a kid. He had a small heart attack when I was thirteen and he decided to get himself into shape. He has been doing well since then.

"So, why didn't you go with Andrea today?" Mom asked, changing the subject.

"She hasn't answered any of my calls." I admitted.

"Is she sick?" Mom sounded worried.

"I don't know. She's not answering any of my calls." I repeated myself.

"That's weird of her." Dad added.

"Yeah, it is." I agreed.

"So, who is this Kora?" Mom asked curiously.

"She's the new neighbor's daughter." I told her.

"Is she pretty?" Dad asked.

"Hector," Mom was offended he asked that. "He has a girlfriend."

"Just answer the question." Dad joked.

"Yeah, I guess." I didn't know what to say. She was very pretty but I didn't want to say too much. Mom would wring my neck if I told her I kissed another girl. She loved Andrea. I loved Andrea too, but right now I was just so confused.

"Well, I'm glad she could keep you company. And I hope everything with you and Andrea is okay." Mom said.

"I hope so too." I confessed.

"Well, boys it's been a long day and I'm ready to turn in." Mom said as she yawned and stretched her arms out.

"Me too," Dad agreed.

"I'll see you boys in the morning." Mom gave me a hug and kissed my forehead before starting up the stairs. "I'll make you both breakfast when I get up." She announced as she made her way up to her room.

THE NEIGHBOR

"Goodnight, Mom," I yelled to her.

"Goodnight, son." She yelled back.

"Goodnight, Dad." I told him and returned to my room. Kora's bedroom light was off, so I knew she was already asleep. It took me a while to finally fall asleep because my brain just wouldn't shut off. Why is Andrea not answering my calls? Did she find someone else? I had to talk to her. I had to know what was going on. I had to tell her I was going to be on TV. She would love to come shopping with me and my mom. She loved helping dress me for special occasions and dances. My eyes started to get heavy, and I could no longer keep them open. I drifted off, thinking of Andrea.

Chapter Twelve

Kora

I walked into Willows and dropped my bookbag behind the counter. Friday night and I wanted to be anywhere besides here, working. Mom and Dad complained about not getting to spend time together, so they ran off to have a date night. I was to clean Willows and lock it up, with the help of Jen of course. They would never leave me in charge of Willows by myself. They still didn't trust me fully. I thought the point of moving here meant forgiveness of all. But hey, what do I know? I'm just a teenager who has a lot to learn. That's what my mom likes to remind me of daily. I swear she hasn't a clue on what it's like to be me. She probably doesn't even remember what it was like being a teenager.

At least my dad has some faith in me. "Give her a chance, Helen," is what he told her when she announced the news, I wasn't allowed to close by myself. "How can we trust her if we don't give her the opportunity to be trusted?"

It was useless though. Mom still didn't cave. "Andrew, this is not up for debate. I said what I said and that is final."

So here I am clearing off tables and washing dishes. You'd think being the owner's daughter I could have been a server or the cashier or something other than the busser. Just goes to show

how much trust my parents actually have in me. I was cleaning off a table when Jen's voice distracted me.

"Hey Kora, would you like to take the next customer to get some practice in?" she offered. She knew she was taking a risk with my parents gone. They would fire her if they knew.

"Um, I'm not sure my mom would want me to." I said nervously.

"We don't have to tell her." She said as she winked. I debated on an answer.

"Sure," I finally agreed. We weren't that busy for a Friday night, so it couldn't hurt.

"Awesome, I'll let you know when the next customers come in, okay?" she said in her usual cheerful voice.

"Okay," I replied. Jen wasn't like the other people in this town. She wasn't judgmental. She didn't see gender or color. It was all about personality with her. She was well liked in our community and actually had her head on straight. She was saving up to get out of this town and travel the world. It was going to take years. Especially if she didn't find a better job than working with Mom and Dad. I know she didn't make much but did well with tips. Jen had the prettiest smile and such beautiful hair. I know that kind of odd to mention but Jen's looked healthy and shiny. My hair was dry and brittle from constantly dying it black. Her brown hair with highlights complimented her caramel skin.

As soon as I got caught up with the dishes, I decided to go sit at the counter and write in my journal. I had already written half a page before the bell on the door rang, telling us we had a customer. I grew excited to finally take someone's order and jumped up from my seat to greet them. As soon as I noticed it was Andrea and her group of friends that walked in, my excitement quickly disappeared. Jen nudged my shoulder and winked. She didn't know how much I dreaded taking Andrea's order. Especially after I had kissed her boyfriend that I hoped she didn't know about. Andrea along with Tyrell, Rocco, and two other females all sat in a booth by the window. I handed them each a menu and a set of silverware.

"What can I get you all to drink?" I asked politely. Andrea noticed it was me and rolled her eyes.

"Water." She said rudely.

"Coke for me." Tyrell responded.

"I'll have the same." Said the blonde girl sitting in between Andrea and the brown-haired girl.

"Coke for me as well."

"I'll have a sweet tea with lemon, please." The brown-haired girl said with a chirpy voice.

"So, water, three Cokes, and one sweet tea with lemon, correct?" I repeated the drink order.

THE NEIGHBOR

"Yes, now hurry along and fetch our drinks." Andrea said without even looking at me. Everyone at the table giggled under their breaths.

"What the hell is her problem," I wondered as I walked to the drink station to get their drinks. Then I remembered I kissed her boyfriend. Krystian must have told her what happened. My face turned red from embarrassment. I felt ashamed of myself. There was no way I could face her now.

"You did great taking their drink orders." Jen said with a big smile on her face. She looked proud of me. And I haven't seen anyone look at me like that in a long time. I knew she was going to be disappointed as soon as I told her I couldn't take their order and why. Before I could mention it to her, we heard a burst of laughter.

"Sounds like they are having a great time." Jen said, peeking around the corner to look at them. I stopped and listened to what they were talking about. Andrea was the one talking, and it sounded like she was reading from something.

"That's when I realized my shorts were missing." She read and everyone started laughing again hysterically.

Wait. That sounds familiar, I thought to myself.

"I have never been so embarrassed in my life." She continued to read and everyone else continued to laugh.

My journal. I remembered leaving it on the table I was sitting at. "NO!" I exclaimed. I ran to the table where Andrea and her friends were sitting at. "STOP! What are you doing?"

I didn't realize Jen was right behind me. "Kora, what's wrong?" she asked, worried.

"She's reading my journal." I cried out. Tears fell from my eyes and now I was even more embarrassed. Everyone looked at Jen whose eyes narrowed, and lips pierced. She was angry and I don't think anyone has ever seen her angry.

"You all need to leave." She ordered them in a stern voice.

"But we didn't even get to order yet." The blonde girl complained. Everyone else sighed in disappointment.

"I don't care, Stacy!" Jen's voice got louder. "Unless you want me to call all your parents and let them know what you all are up to, I suggest you leave right now and don't come back."

Andrea rolled her eyes. "Let's get out of here. This place is lame anyways since the new owners took over." I knew Andrea was only trying to hurt me more with the comment she made, but little did she know I cared more about my journal than I did about my parents being lame. One by one they all scooted out of the booth. Andrea was the last one.

"Andrea." Jen reached her hand out to Andrea as soon as she stood up. Andrea looked at her confused. "The book."

Andrea rolled her eyes and handed Jen my book. We watched as they all walked out of Willows.

Jen handed me my book. "I'm sorry they did that to you. Some people have no respect."

"Thank you for getting it back for me."

"No problem at all." She smiled at me. "You let me know if they give you any more trouble."

"I will."

"It's dead as hell in here. Let's start cleaning up and shut down early. I'm sure your parents wouldn't mind since it's only an hour early."

"Okay." I answered.

"Hey Jon, shut it down." Jen shouted to the cook who was still in the kitchen. "We are going home early."

"Yes ma'am." Del peeked out the door that led to the kitchen. He was a big guy with a long beard. He had to be in his fifties. My mom made him wear a net over his head and beard both. She was very strict. I heard when mom first got here, they had gotten into a disagreement and said some very bad things to each other. Mom could have fired him, but she chose not to. He was just a person trying to make a living. They get along excellently now. I wish she could be so forgiving with me.

I started refilling up the salt and pepper jars on the tables after I wiped them all down again. I knew it was going to take Del and Jen a while to get the back cleaned up. I tried to keep myself busy by thinking about the embarrassment that happened earlier with Andrea. If she had known what happened between Krystian and I she would have said something, and I thanked my lucky stars that she only got that far in my journal.

"Hey Kora," Jen's voice startled me.

"Yeah Jen?" I pretended like she just didn't scare me.

"Do you think you can take the trash out while we finish up back here?"

"Sure."

"Thank you so much sweetie." She smiled. "It shouldn't take us much longer."

Jen returned to the kitchen to help finish helping Jon. I grabbed the two big bags of garbage that were sitting in front of the back door. I struggled to get the door open and hold the bags at the same time. I realized just then I needed to work out because I was weak. It took me a couple of minutes to get the bags into the big dumpster that was taller than me. I stood there with my hands on my hips trying to catch my breath but at the same time proud of myself. I heard giggling in the distance. At first, I hesitated to check who it was. I've seen a lot of scary movies. The voices sounded familiar, so I decided to look. Standing behind Willows under a streetlamp in the alley were Andrea and Tyrell. I stood there for a second making sure my eyes weren't deceiving me. Tyrell had his arms around Andrea, and he pulled her closer to him and Andrea wrapped her arms around his neck. They began to kiss.

"Kora, you back here?" Jen's voice startled me once again. "Oh, here you are." I looked at Jen then back at Andrea and Tyrell. They both looked at me scared. They knew I would tell Krystian what I saw.

"We're all done." Jen said cheerfully. She couldn't see them because the dumpster was in the way.

"Okay, I'm ready." I told her and hurried back into Willows.

"Are you okay?" Jen asked.

"Yeah, I'm just anxious to get home." I lied.

"Okay, well do you still need a ride home?" she asked. I had forgotten that my parents asked her to take me home after we closed.

"Yeah, thanks." I told her. I was scared that if I walked home Tyrell and Andrea would come after me or something, now that I knew their secret.

Chapter Thirteen

Krystian

It was finally Monday morning, and I knew Andrea would be at school. She never misses unless she was really sick or there was an emergency at home. I was feeling nervous and anxious to see her. It's weird, a girl that I have dated over three years and right now I feel like we were strangers. I have never had a problem talking to her about anything and I feel like now we were just slipping away from each other.

As I strolled down the hall towards Andrea's locker, I noticed several students running in the same direction as I was walking.

"I think they are going to fight!" A nerdy boy in glasses said excitedly.

"Andrea is going to kill her." His friend said to him.

"What is going on?" I yelled to them as they were passing by.

The nerdy boy in glasses barely stopped. "Andrea and that new girl are about to fight!" He yelled back as he turned the corner.

"Kora?" I said to myself out loud. Why would Andrea try to fight Kora? Does she know about Saturday with Kora? Does she know that I kissed her? I have to stop this. I hurried around the corner to where a crowd of students were standing. I could hear Andrea talking to Kora sternly.

THE NEIGHBOR

"You keep your mouth shut or else!" She ordered.

"Or else what?" Kora said not sounding scared at all. I pushed my way through the crowd. I made it to where they were standing and just as I did, Andrea pushed Kora and Kora fell on the floor hard. Everyone started laughing at her.

"Andrea!" I yelled at her. "What are you doing?" I reached my hand out for Kora to grab and she did so. I pulled her up off the ground. "Are you okay?" I asked her. She nodded her head yes but didn't say anything.

"You have got to be kidding me right now!" Andrea was upset.

"What is going on here?" Principal Klein's deep voice came somewhere through the crowd. "Everyone! Get to class now!" His voice was stern. Students didn't hesitate to do what he ordered them to do. I grabbed Andrea's arm and pulled her through the students scattering around us. I didn't want her to get in trouble.

"What are you doing?" she asked upset. "Let go of me!" She jerked her arm from my hand and stopped walking. We had made it into the guy's bathroom. It was empty thankfully, but she wasn't pleased this is where I brought her. "Why did you bring me in here?"

"I'm trying to help you." I told her. "I don't understand why you are treating me like this!" I just came out and said it.

"Treating you how?" she chuckled.

"Going after Kora because of me. Ignoring me all weekend."

"You think this is about you?" she laughed sarcastically. "You wish this was about you!"

"Then what is this about?" I asked confused.

"It's none of your business." She said with her lips pursed.

"You are my business, Andrea! I love you and I don't even know what the hell is going on with you anymore." I tried to explain.

"Well maybe if you had more time for me, you would know what was going on, but you'd rather take another girl with you to hang out." She fired back.

"I tried to call you and even went to your house, and you ignored me. What else was I supposed to do?" I knew she would be angry about me hanging out with another girl. I just didn't want to go alone, and I never planned on kissing Kora. It just sort have happened.

"Go alone and not take another girl." Her face was turning red from anger.

"Don't turn this around on me, Andrea," I began to say.

"I'm not turning anything around, Krystian, this is your fault." Her eyes wet. I could tell she was hiding something. But what? I had to get it out of her but I'm so angry with her. The way she was treating me was like it's all my fault. Why won't she just admit what she has done?

THE NEIGHBOR

"You weren't answering my calls or texts before I even left to the lake. So no, it's not my fault that I took Kora it is your fault that you weren't home and ignored me all day." I repeated myself.

Andrea didn't say a word. She just stood there with her arms crossed and eyebrows narrowed. Her lips moved slightly like she was about to say something, but no words came out of her mouth. She was holding back, and I didn't know why. Andrea never held back from telling me anything. Especially, when she was angry with me. What is she hiding? What does she not want me to know? I was getting impatient waiting for an answer. I knew her silence was a message. I couldn't do this anymore. I couldn't be with someone who kept secrets from me.

"Are you going to say anything to me?" I asked her calmly. Andrea wouldn't even look at me. Her eyes just kept gazing around the room, ignoring me. "Okay Andrea, I'll give you what you want."

Andrea finally looked at me curious about what I was about to say.

"We are done." I was hoping she would be hurt by the words I said and beg me to stay. At least that's what I would have done if she dumped me. She just stared at me blankly. I thought I saw her eyes begin to water but she held them back. Maybe she thought I was bluffing. Even I thought I was bluffing, but by her reaction I knew this was for real. "By the way, I kissed Kora." I added just to try to hurt her.

Andrea's hand hit hard across my face. It came as a shock. I wasn't expecting that from her at all.

"You're going to pay for that!" She threatened before storming out of the bathroom. Andrea was a small girl, but she could throw a punch. My jaw hurt like hell and if she left a bruise my mom would freak out.

I tried to pretend that Andrea and I breaking up wasn't a big deal, but it was. I didn't want to be at school so I called my mom and told her I was sick, hoping she would break me free from this hell of a school. She just so happened to be out having lunch with my dad. Which I found odd. I thought divorced people tried to stay away from each other. They were spending a lot more time together than they had when they were married. I wasn't going to complain about it though. I was still hopeful they would get back together. Maybe Andrea and I would get back together as well. I saw her in a couple of classes we shared, and she seemed unbothered about the breakup. Was this what she had wanted this whole time?

I tried to think back to when I first noticed she had changed. It was right after Kameron was killed. She was there for me during the funeral and afterwards but that's when she started to drift away slowly. My mom kept me on a tight leash, and she was right, I didn't get to spend a whole lot of time with her. Had she moved on to someone else? The whole school was talking about the almost fight between Andrea and Kora. No one mentioned me kissing Kora so what was the fight about? It had to be serious. I had never seen Andrea so angry with someone and I knew if she knew what really happened at the lake with Kora, she wouldn't have stopped with one punch. I had to talk to Kora and find out what's going on.

95

Chapter Fourteen

Kora

"Kora, wait!" I heard Krystian yelling behind me. "I need to talk to you." I turned around to see him running towards me.

"What do you want?" I asked rudely. I was so upset with him. He hadn't tried to talk to me all day. He didn't even try to stick up for me with Andrea. Not even a simple apology.

"You're mad at me too?" he asked, trying to catch his breath.

"Should I not be?" I asked.

"What did I do that was so wrong?" he complained.

"You were just going to let your girlfriend beat me up without saying a word to her. And you expect me not to be mad at you?" I explained with my voice getting louder and louder. I noticed some students had stopped and stared at us, thinking something about to happen.

"I wouldn't have let it get that far. I promise." He tried to convince me.

"She pushed me to the ground, Krystian!" I reminded him. "Everybody laughed at me."

"I helped you up." He pointed out. I couldn't believe him. Did he really think that would have made it all better?

"Your girlfriend embarrassed me in front of the whole school, and you just let her."

"I pulled her away from you." He argued back.

"What do you want, Krystian?" I asked again, hoping I would get an answer this time. He clearly wasn't understanding the point I was trying to make.

"Why were you two arguing in the first place?" he asked.

I hesitated to tell him. Why should I tell him? It's his girlfriend's place to tell him what's going on, not mine. "Why don't you ask your girlfriend?" I finally said.

"She isn't my girlfriend anymore." He looked at the ground. A part of me felt relieved that he finally got rid of her but the other part of me felt sad for him because he looked sad.

"I'm sorry to hear that," I said, not really meaning it. "I hope it wasn't my fault." I tried to sound sincere even though I didn't care for Andrea at all. I knew she was two timing Krystian, and he deserved better than her.

"No. It was my own fault." He replied with his head down. I couldn't help but fall for it. I wasn't so upset with him anymore. "What was the incident about?" he asked me again.

I didn't want to tell him it was because I saw his girlfriend kissing another guy. That would only destroy him even more. If Andrea had told him about Tyrell, then he wouldn't be asking me about it now.

"It was over an incident that happened at the Willows Friday night." I told him. It wasn't a lie, so I didn't feel too guilty.

"What happened?" he asked concerned.

"It's not important and I don't want to talk about it." I wined. I didn't want him to know and if he kept talking and asking questions, I knew I would end up telling him everything he wanted to know. I didn't want to hurt him more than he already was.

"Do you think I could come by later?" he looked at me with sadness in his eyes. I felt bad for him. "I just don't want to be alone, and I could really use the company. Your company." He added. Did he just ask me to hang out? The inner me jumped for joy with excitement but my brain told me to act naturally. He just broke up with his girlfriend, Kora, and he just wants a friend. Stop getting your hopes up. He's the first boy I ever had a crush on, and I didn't know how to act around him sometimes. Especially after the kiss we shared together.

"Yeah sure," I tried to not sound like my inner self wasn't doing flips right now.

"Great," he gave me a small grin. "Can I walk with you home?" he asked.

"I don't see why not. We're neighbors so we're headed the same direction." I snorted and was instantly embarrassed.

He chuckled at me, and I felt the heat coming from my face even more. A part of me wished he didn't notice it. I was too embarrassed to say anything. Why do I keep making a fool out of myself in front of him? "That was cute." He smiled at me.

I knew he was just saying that to make me feel good. No way in hell was that cute. Especially coming from me. I quickly turned away, gripping my bookbag straps tighter from my frustration. Ugh, he's going to realize what a loser I really am and never wants to speak to me again. I just know it.

"Wait up," he was trying hard to keep up with me. "Why are you walking so fast?"

"Sorry," I said not wanting him to know the truth. I was trying to get home as fast as I could, so I didn't have time to embarrass myself again. But knowing me it was bound to happen.

"You're good," he said as I slowed down so he could keep up with me.

"Krystian!" We both stopped walking and turned to see who the voice belonged to that had yelled out his name. It was Rocco, along with Tyrell and Andrea walking towards us.

"You go ahead and go," he looked concerned as he told me. "I'll catch up with you." Before I could say anything, he started walking towards them. I turned to walk away feeling disappointed that he wasn't walking me home. I started walking fast again. I just wanted to get home and get this day over with. I heard yelling behind me and turned to see what was going on. Krystian and Rocco were face to face arguing.

"You put hands on her?" Rocco yelled. They were so close that if they moved the slightest towards each other they would kiss.

I didn't know what I should do. Should I go back and help him? What could I do? That horrible night with Terra popped into my head. I would only make things worse. But if I do nothing, would he think of me as a coward?

"I never touched her!" Krystian yelled back at him. Rocco raised his right fist and hit Krystian hard in the face, knocking him to the ground.

I gasped.

I couldn't just leave him. I had to do something. But what? What could I do?

"Stay away from her!" Rocco threatened. They all walked off, leaving Krystian on the ground bleeding.

I ran to him. "Are you alright?" I asked concerned. I tried to help him up, but he pushed me away.

"Stop!" He yelled.

"I was just trying to help." I pointed out, now angry that he was treating me like this.

"I don't need your help." He was angry. I could tell in his voice. I knew he wasn't angry at me, but at Rocco and the situation that just occurred. He stood up on his own as I stood close by him ready to help anyway I could if he needed me to. He looked in the direction they were all walking. His stare was evil. I could see the hatred he had in his eyes. It honestly scared me. I never wanted to be on his bad side. I hardly knew him.

"They are going to pay for that." He said under his breath. I looked at them and then back at him. What did he mean? Was he going to hurt them? The way he was staring as they walked away, I wouldn't put it past him. No, Krystian wasn't that type. He couldn't be. He was a good person. He couldn't hurt anybody. Or so I thought.

Chapter Fifteen

Krystian

I wiped the steam off the shower mirror and looked at the black eye Rocco left me. I was so furious. Why didn't I get my ass up and fight him? I laid there like a coward in front of Andrea and Kora. They both knew I was a loser by now. Well, I take that back. Andrea already knew I was a loser. But Kora didn't. I was so mean to her, and she didn't deserve that. She still walked me home. It was a quiet walk. We didn't say one word to each other the whole way. I wanted to say a lot to her, but I knew she was thinking I was a nobody the whole time. My mom flipped out when she saw my eye.

"I'm calling your father and we are going to march down to that school and make sure he gets punished for doing what he did to you!" She said angrily.

"Mom, no!" I was embarrassed. "Why stir up more trouble?"

"He gave you a black eye because you wouldn't do his homework!" She said, trying to plead with me. "He is a bully Krystian, and I will not let my son be bullied."

I lied to her about the reason behind the black eye. She didn't need to know. Why Andrea lied to Tyrell and Rocco, I don't know. What was she really hiding? I knew she was up to no good. I just didn't know what she was doing. I knew she wouldn't talk to me even if I tried. Now she has two bodyguards by her side all the time. When did she start hanging out with Tyrell and Rocco like that? I wanted answers and I wanted them now. I had to figure out what Kora and Andrea were fighting about. I had to know the truth.

"I'm fine, Mom." I finally said to her.

"If you're brother was here this wouldn't have happened." She said under her breath.

"But he isn't!" My blood started to boil. My hands balled up into fists.

"What is wrong with you, Krystian?" My mom had a horrified look on her face.

"I'm tired of it, Mom. I'm tired of living in his shadow. If it wasn't for him, I wouldn't be going through this now!" I said too much. I knew by the look in her eyes that several questions were about to follow.

"What are you talking about?" her eyes were starting to glisten. "What is really going on, Krystian?"

"Nothing Mom." I tried to walk away, regretting I ever said anything. I just couldn't keep it bottled up anymore.

"Don't walk away from me, Krystian!" She yelled. I didn't stop. Instead, I walked to my room and locked the door behind me. I turned my Bluetooth on and connected it to my speaker that once belonged to Kameron. My mom was knocking on my door.

"Krystian, talk to me!" She demanded but I didn't say a word. Instead, I went through my playlist and hit play on the song that I knew would help calm myself down. Disturbed always did that for me. My mom continued to knock so I turned the volume to max to drown her out. I laid on my bed just thinking. Thinking about everything. Thinking about Andrea and how we ended up in this mess. Thinking about Kameron and what we would be doing if he was here. Thinking about Kora and how I wanted to get to know her better. I wanted to be more than friends with her. I wanted her more than I ever wanted Andrea. So why was I so upset with Andrea dumping me? I loved her. Didn't I? Not if I kissed Kora, right? Everything was so confusing to me. I drifted off with none of my questions answered.

As I looked at myself in the mirror, I hardly recognized myself anymore. What have I become? How did I get here? I knew exactly how I got here. I just wasn't about to admit it yet. My mom had already left for work by the time I woke up. I was relieved I didn't have to face her right now. It's not that I couldn't answer her questions, it's just that I didn't want to. Not right now anyways. I knew leaving her in the dark was only destroying her more, but I didn't have a choice right now. I got dressed and noticed that Kora's bedroom light was still on. She must still be awake, writing in her journal. I wondered if she was writing about me. How I let Rocco punk me the way he did. I grabbed my phone off the nightstand and sent her a text message.

You awake?

THE NEIGHBOR

She replied instantly.

Yes

Come over

K

Within minutes, she was at my door wearing black sweats and a black spaghetti strapped shirt. Her black hair was in a messy bun. She was cute. I couldn't hide the smile on my face. I was surprised she even came over considering how late it was.

"Hey." I opened the door and motioned for her to come in.

"Is everything okay?" she asked concerned as she walked in.

I closed the door behind her. "Of course." I said, giving her a confused look. "Why wouldn't it be?"

"I heard yelling earlier. Then your music was blaring."

"Oh, that was nothing." I lied. "Me and my mom had a disagreement."

"Me and my mom do that all the time. I swear I hate it."

"That's a mom for you." I chuckled. For some reason I felt nervous. I haven't felt nervous around a girl in years. Three years to be exact. When I first met Andrea.

"So, what's going on?" she asked, changing the subject.

"Nothing."

"Oh," she looked confused again. "I thought you asked me over here because something was wrong."

"I just didn't want to be alone." I admitted. "Is that a problem?"

"No," she answered quickly. "I just wanted to know why I snuck out of the house."

"I didn't know you were such a rebel." I teased her.

"I'm usually not. My parents usually have me on a tight leash." She was being serious. I don't think she realized I was only joking with her.

"Same here since my brother's passing. My mom has locked me up in this house."

"Yeah, it gets suffocating after a while. I mean we're teenagers, we should be allowed to live and make mistakes. They can't shelter us forever."

"Right," she made sense. "Do you want anything to drink?"

"Water is fine." She answered softly. Her voice was always low and soft. She seemed fragile. I walked to the kitchen and grabbed bottled water out of the fridge and grabbed myself a Coke. I walked back and handed it to her.

"We can go to the living room if you want to." I offered.

"Okay."

She followed me closely as we made our way to the living room. I sat down on the couch, and she sat down at the other end of the couch. I scooted closer to her, and she looked uncomfortable. I didn't move away. I wanted her to be vulnerable. I don't know why. I guess I wanted to see how she was under pressure.

"How are you liking it here?" I asked hoping I could get her to open up like she did at the pizza joint.

"It's okay. I'm still trying to get used to it." She said nervously.

"It's okay here, I guess. I can't wait to leave though."

"Must not be that great if you want to leave." She said.

"I didn't always feel that way." I confessed. "But after Kameron, I just think it's best that I leave here. Way too many memories."

"I get that." She gave me a half smile. "What do you think happened?"

I was confused by her question at first but after a few seconds it clicked that she was talking about Kameron's death. "I wish I knew."

"Do you have any clues on who you think did it?" Kora asked, eager to know. It was the first time I saw her face light up.

"I think I know, I just can't prove it." I admitted.

"Who?" she sat up straight and no longer looked nervous.

"The obvious. Tyrell and Rocco."

"I can see that." She said as she untwisted the cap on her water bottle and finally took a drink.

"What do you mean by that?" I waited until after she was finished with her drink to ask.

"They are the popular boys and the star football players. I'm sure they have most of this town wrapped around their fingers."

"Is it that obvious?' I chuckled.

"What makes you think they were involved?" she asked curiously.

"Just because of what happened earlier that day. I mean I don't have any evidence or anything."

"What happened earlier that day?" Her body seemed more relaxed than when she got here. She seemed to be interested in Kameron's death which I felt was odd. She didn't even know him. I wanted to desperately change the subject.

"I'll make you a deal," I offered.

"What kind of a deal?" she asked curiously.

"If you tell me why you and Andrea were arguing, I'll tell you everything I know about Kameron's death and what I think happened."

Kora's eyes widened. She hesitated and her body was no longer relaxed. She became stiff again and she was back to uncomfortable.

"I don't know Krystian." She finally said. "It's not my place to say."

What did she mean by that? Why wouldn't she just tell me what it was about? "I promise I won't be upset with you whatever it is."

"Fine." She finally gave in, taking a deep breath in before she spoke. "I saw Tyrell and Andrea kissing behind Willows, and she saw me watching them. She threatened if I told you she would make sure I got what was coming to me."

My blood started to boil again. Sweat started to form on the top of my forehead. I wanted to hurt Tyrell and Andrea. "I can't believe she did this to me again." I blurted out.

"Again?" Kora had her usual curious look on her face.

"It's nothing. It was a long time ago." I stated.

"She cheated on you before?" her eyes widened in disbelief.

"Yeah, but I forgave her. It was a long time ago and I thought we moved past it. Tyrell is the type of guy that's always going to get what he wants, even if it belongs to someone else. Which is why I think he had something to do with Kameron's death. He and Rocco were bullying Samuel earlier that day and we stopped them. Tyrell was pissed because he knew my brother would have kicked his ass."

"Wow!" Kora looked shocked.

"Yeah, but I can't prove anything and even if I could, who is to say the police would do anything about it?"

"Why wouldn't they?" she sat up straight and her eyes narrowed like she was upset.

"Rocco's dad is the Sheriff." I explained.

"You're kidding right?" her eyes grew wide with shock.

"Nope." I confirmed.

"That's not fair to you or your parents." She said.

"I know but we can't do anything about it. I tried to tell my mom, but the town has her convinced it was a stranger that was just passing through that night."

"So why don't you find the evidence that you need?" she suggested.

"How?" I didn't think I could find any evidence. I'm not that smart. I wouldn't even know where to start.

"I can help you." She offered. Her eyes lit up with excitement.

"Again, how? They will never confess anything to me." I pointed out. "I have a black eye from Rocco if you hadn't noticed."

Kora looked disappointed. "I'll think of something." She mumbled under her breath.

"The police will figure it out. It's too dangerous trying to pretend we're something we're not. I don't want you to get hurt, Kora."

Kora looked up at me. I could see a smile forming on her lips. "You don't want me to get hurt?"

"No, I don't." I smiled back at her. Her face started to turn red. She looked away hoping to hide it. "I do care about you, Kora. I know you just moved here but honestly, you're the only friend I have right now."

"That can't be true." She said in disbelief.

"Andrea is the popular one. They are all her friends not mine." I admitted. "Now that we aren't together, none of them will pay me any attention."

"Are you going to miss them?"

"No, I think I like being in the shadows more." I admitted.

"Yeah, me too." She made a small chuckle.

"Would you go out with me?" I blurted out.

Kora looked nervous and she was having a hard time trying to talk. I smiled knowing I made her disconcerted. I waited patiently for her answer as she tried to give me one. Her words were all scattered around as she tried not to stutter. It was the cutest thing ever. The smile plastered on my face grew bigger and bigger and the more it did I know it made her even more nervous.

"W... Wh... why?" she finally formed a word out of her mouth.

I was expecting her words to be yes, not why. "Because I like you, Kora. I've liked you since I first laid eyes on you." I admitted to her. "Otherwise, I would have never kissed you that day at the lake. I would never have asked you to go with me, but I wanted to spend time with you and get to know you a little better. You are so much different from the girls around here."

"And that's a good thing?" she asked. I could tell she had low self-esteem. That's the one personality trait I didn't like about her. She was beautiful. Why couldn't she see that?

"That is a good thing. Girls around here are snobby and selfish." I knew Kora was different. She was quiet and mysterious. She definitely had secrets and I was going to uncover them all.

"I'll be your girlfriend!" She blurted out with excitement. She had the biggest smile on her face. It was beautiful, she was beautiful.

I heard this voice in my head that told me to kiss her. Kiss her now! So, I listened. I leaned in towards her and put my hand behind her head and pulled her toward me until our lips met. The warmth of her mouth on mine did something to me that was completely different from when I kissed Andrea. She didn't pull away from me, so I knew I was doing the right thing. Excitement rushed through my body, and I didn't want to stop kissing her. I slowly moved forward, and she went back. Before I had realized I was on top of her. I put my hand on her waist and I slowly moved it under her shirt. Her skin was so soft. Just how I imagined it would be. As I moved my hand up, she pulled away from me.

THE NEIGHBOR

Kora looked horrified and I was confused. "I have to get home." She said as she sat up. I moved out of her way.

"Is everything okay?" I asked concerned and confused about what just happened.

"I have to go" is all she said as she ran out the front door.

I continued to sit on the couch wondering why she just left like that. I thought she was enjoying herself. I thought we were on the same page. Does this mean she didn't want to be my girlfriend?

Chapter Sixteen

Kora

I wanted to be Krystian's girlfriend more than anything. I just wasn't ready to do what I knew he wanted to do. My body was telling me to give myself to him. It's your job to make him happy. He's your boyfriend now. But my heart was telling me to slow down. I was so scared to face him. Was he angry with me? Will he break up with me? What if he doesn't want a girlfriend that isn't going to do the things he wanted me to do? I felt like such an idiot. I had a boyfriend for a whole damn minute. Literally! That had to be some kind of record. Then the sudden thought of my parents popped into my head. I knew I shouldn't have told him yes until I asked permission from my parents first. They would have ended the relationship to begin with. Well, I guess I did that on my own.

I was starting to feel sick from all the overthinking. Daylight was already starting to peek through my window. I hadn't realized it was this early. I had been up all night overthinking. I saw Krystian's lights go out shortly after I ran home. He didn't seem to lose any sleep over what happened. Why would he? Why would he waste his time with me anyways? I was a nobody. I wasn't anything special. What did he see in me? Was this one of those pranks or bets like in one of those movies where the guy gets paid to date the girl or loses a bet and has to date her. Great, now I'm overthinking some more. My eyes became harder to keep open. I have to sleep. Maybe I could think clearly if I got some sleep.

I awoke to a knocking sound on the door. Trying to wipe the sleep out of my eyes I heard the door creak open. My dad poked his head in. "Are you awake?" he asked softly.

"Yeah, Dad, I am. What time is it?" I asked.

"It's just after 5 p.m." He opened the door completely and took a step in.

"You mean I missed school? I didn't mean to oversleep." I confessed, hoping I wasn't in trouble.

"Mom suggested you stay home. She didn't think you were feeling good. Also, she got you something."

"Mom got me something?" I asked confused. When has my mom ever gone out of her way to get me anything besides clothes and hygiene stuff? She hated buying me things.

"She is really trying, Kora. Just give her a chance." Dad stated before handing me a box.

I grabbed the box from him and examined it. It was a cell phone. "What? Really?" I asked excited and shocked at the same time.

Dad didn't respond. He just looked at me and smiled. I had a feeling this was more of his idea than mom's. She banned me from having a phone and now she was just handing one over?

And letting me sleep in? Usually, she would be down my neck. Maybe she really was trying?

"Thank you, dad, so much!" I climbed out of bed and gave him a big hug before sitting back down and ripping the box open.

"You are welcome." He smiled. "Oh, before I forget, there is a boy at the door for you." He said.

"A boy?" I asked confused.

He raised his eyebrows and pursed his lips. "Yeah, a boy. You might want to get rid of him before your mother gets home. You know how she is going to overreact." He said before closing my bedroom door as he walked out.

"Krystian." I said out loud before jumping out of bed and running to my closet. I grabbed a t-shirt and threw it over my messy hair and grabbed some black jeans with holes in them out of my dresser drawer. I pulled my sweatpants off and slid my jeans on. I then hurried down the stairs as I attempted to fix my hair. I managed to miss a step and down I went, hitting the floor hard. My dad must have heard me cry out. He rushed to where I was and grabbed my arm to help me up.

"What happened?" he asked concerned.

Before I could reply to him, I heard another voice. "Are you okay?" it was Krystian, and he was just as worried as my dad was. Once again, I could feel the heat on my face, and I knew I was the reddest I have ever been. I felt so embarrassed and humiliated.

"I... I... I'm fine." I managed to speak although it was a struggle getting the words out. I wanted to run back to my room and lock the door behind me. Why was I constantly making a fool of myself in front of him?

"You are bleeding a little bit. Let's get this arm cleaned up." He led the way and Krystian followed closely behind us.

"Dad, I'm okay." I said as I pulled my arm away from him. He ignored me and opened a drawer and reached for a clean dish towel.

"Let your dad help you." Krystian said, not making the situation less humiliating. "Do you have a first aid kit?" he asked my dad.

My dad's eyes lit up as he remembered we had one of those. "Yes, in the bathroom. In the cabinet." He told Krystian and Krystian was off to find it.

"It's really not that big of a deal." I shouted to him as he ran up the stairs. He ignored me. My dad turned the kitchen faucet on and wet the dish towel. He gently patted where I had scraped my elbow. "I really am fine, Dad." I tried to convince him. He ignored me as he continued to pat. It stung a little, but it wasn't a big deal.

"So, who's the boy?" he asked, not looking up at me.

"His name is Krystian." I answered.

"Does he go to your school?" he asked.

"Yeah, and he just so happens to be out neighbor." I added.

My dad looked up at me with a serious look in his eyes. "Is he your boyfriend?"

I grew nervous and scared at the same time. I knew my dad would overreact if I told him the truth. He would then tell my mom and she would literally turn into a maniac. I think my dad already knew the answer to his question by how hesitant I was. Before either one of us could say anything, Krystian returned with the first aid kit. I let out a sigh of relief.

"Found it," he said as he looked at me with a small smile.

My dad grabbed the kit from Krystian and opened it up, looking for the antibiotic cream. "Thank you." He said to Krystian. Krystian just smiled back at him in return. Everyone was quiet until my dad was done doctoring me up. I felt like I was eight years old again and I had fallen off my bike. My dad would always be quick to get the first aid kit and patch me up. Mom would tell him to just leave it. I needed to stop being babied and it would toughen me up. Dad didn't care. He'd clean the scrape off and place a band-aid wherever I needed it. Just as he has done this time.

"All better." He said as he threw the band-aid wrapper in the trash and closed up the kit.

"Thanks, Dad."

"No problem." He smiled and kissed my forehead. "I don't think we have been formally introduced." He turned to Krystian and reached out his hand.

"Krystian," he placed his hand in my dad's hand and shook it.

"Kora says you live next door." My dad asked Krystian.

"Yeah, I do. With my mom." He replied.

"No dad?"

"Dad!" I scolded him.

"What?" He didn't see a problem with his question.

"Divorced. But he still comes around." Krystian assured him.

"So, what brings you over today?" My dad glanced at me then back at Krystian.

"Oh, I needed to talk to Kora about an assignment we have in history class." He lied.

"Do you two have a lot of classes together?" My dad was just being nosey now.

"Dad," I said trying to attempt to make him stop asking so many questions.

"What?" He looked at me like he was doing nothing wrong. "I'm just trying to get to know the neighbor kid."

"We have a couple of classes together." Krystian didn't seem to mind. He knew exactly what to say.

"She isn't doing your homework for you is she?" he asked seriously. I rolled my eyes, and I knew that he had seen me do it.

"No... not at all, sir," Krystian started to sound nervous.

"Dad, I'm going to walk Krystian out and discuss the history assignment he's talking about. Okay?" I needed to get Krystian out of the house before my mom came home and saw him. That would be a pleasant surprise for him for sure.

"Sure thing." He smiled at me. "If you need anything let me know. History was my major in college."

"Really?" Krystian asked curiously.

I cleared my throat trying to get his attention. I was trying to save him from the story of how he and my mother met.

My dad's eyes lit up. He loved talking about his college days. When his life was perfect. Before I came along. "True story. I was the top of my class. That's where I met Kora's mother." He pointed out. I didn't feel like listening to this story again.

"Dad," I interrupted him. "I'm sure Krystian would love to hear how you and mom met, but this assignment is due by the end of the week." I lied to him.

My dad looked at Krystian. "Some other time?"

"Sure." Krystian responded although I felt he was just being courteous.

I walked with Krystian out the front door. I could feel my dad's eyes on me the whole way out. I didn't dare to look behind me to know for sure. I sat on the steps feeling nervous. Was he here to break up with me? I wouldn't blame him if he did. Krystian sat down beside me. He nervously grabbed my hand and held it. I grew even more nervous. I could feel the sweat starting to form on my forehead. I didn't look at Krystian and he didn't look at me.

"I don't want you to be upset about last night." He began to say as he looked everywhere, besides me. "I shouldn't have tried to pressure you and I'm sorry if I made you feel like you had to do it or you owed me something. I really am sorry."

It took me a moment to respond. I didn't know how to respond. I wasn't expecting an apology. I was expecting to get dumped. "I'm not upset." I confessed. "I was scared, and I freaked out. I'm sorry for running away the way that I did and not explaining myself to you first."

"You don't have to explain yourself to me." He said almost immediately. "I was the jerk and in the wrong. I should have asked you first not the other way around." He finally looked at me and smiled. I returned the smile, and he leaned in and kissed my forehead. I didn't know what to say or even what to think. I was certain he was going to be upset but he was such a gentleman about the whole situation.

"When I'm ready I will let you know." I said to him a little louder than a whisper.

"Have you told your parents yet?" he asked me.

"No, have you told yours?" I asked.

"Not yet either. I'm still dreading talking to my mom. After our fight yesterday with the whole black eye situation, I've been trying my hardest to avoid her." He explained.

"I'm not sure how my parents would react so if you don't mind can I not tell them right away?" I asked nervously.

"Um I guess." He sounded unsure. "But you will tell them eventually, right?"

"Of course, I will. Just not today." I told him although I wasn't sure I would ever tell them. Maybe my dad first, then slowly move into telling my mom. She was stricter than my dad and she would overact like she always did.

"We should hang out today. Just you and me." He suggested.

"What would you like to do?" I asked.

"Not sure," he said. "What are you into to?"

"I like writing, reading, music, art, just about anything really."

"What did you and your friend Terra use to do when you hung out?" he asked.

"We just mostly hung out at either one of our houses or walked around the neighborhood." I thought back and realized we never did anything interesting. We were just a couple of boring people, but we always seemed to have fun in each other's company.

"Well how about I make us some plans this evening?" he offered.

"Okay," I was excited. This was my first real date.

"Just be ready by seven and I'll come pick you up. Is that okay?"

"Sure."

"I gotta get back home. I'll see you at seven then?" He wanted to be sure.

"Yes, seven, I'll be here." I said nervously.

He kissed my forehead and stood up to walk away. I waited until he was out of sight before standing up and returning into the house. My dad was standing there waiting for me as I entered.

"Not your boyfriend huh?" he looked upset.

The smile on my face disappeared instantly. "I'm sorry, Dad." I apologized knowing it wouldn't make a difference. "He asked me last night and I wasn't sure it was real."

"You know your mother isn't going to approve, right?"

"Please don't tell her, daddy." I begged as I tried to play the daddy's girl card like it would actually work.

"Oh, I'm not telling her anything." He smirked. "You are."

"Ugh!" I was getting frustrated. I really liked him, and I knew my mom would end this before it could really start. "I will daddy. But will you give me some time?" I asked him. Maybe I could hide it from her for a while.

"If you are serious about this boy then you shouldn't have to keep him a secret. That's not fair to him at all."

What my dad said made a lot of sense. As much as I didn't want to admit that to him. "I know and I'll tell her soon. You know how Mom is though. She wouldn't understand and she never takes my feelings into consideration.

"Your mom loves you, Kora. She just has a funny way of showing it." He confessed.

"She sure does." I replied sarcastically. "I'm going to shower." I told him before walking away. He said something to me as I walked off, but I didn't hear him. I had to figure out a way to make my mom see that I have really changed. Where she can forgive my past and see I'm not the evil child she portrays me to be. I wanted so much to be with Krystian and the only person that could stand in my way of that happening was my evil mother.

Chapter Seventeen

Krystian

It was two hours before my first date with Kora. I wanted this to be special. I never imagined going on a date with anyone besides Andrea. So, as expected I was nervous as hell. I didn't want to scare her away and wanted to make a good impression. So, I called my dad for advice.

"I'm nervous, Dad."

"That's okay, son. Tell me about this new girl."

"She's beautiful. Looking in her eyes you would get lost in them. She's mysterious. She's everything I'm not used to. If that makes sense."

I could hear my dad giggle on the other end of the line. "Well, she does sound interesting."

"I need advice, Dad." I was starting to panic.

He laughed at me again.

"Why do you think this is funny?" I asked, not understanding what was so funny to him.

"I have never heard you like this," he finally admitted. "I think it's funny."

"Dad! No, it's not funny at all." I was getting frustrated. "Will you please just help me out here?" I begged.

"Take her somewhere special."

"Like where?" I interrupted. I was starting to get impatient. My dad wasn't taking this as seriously as I was.

"Let me finish, Krystian."

"Sorry, go ahead." I apologized.

"Take her to a place that's meaningful to you both. Like the place you met or where you like to hang out together. Somewhere that you have been together or a place she likes or maybe you like. Just make it special and if she isn't impressed then maybe she isn't the one for you."

"Dad!"

"Sorry kiddo. You're a great kid and anyone would be lucky to be with you."

"Andrea didn't feel lucky." I quickly grew sad just thinking about her. Wondering what she a Tyrell were doing. Was she laughing at all his stupid jokes? Or was she annoyed with him already?

"I never liked her anyways." Dad admitted.

It came as a shock to me because I thought everybody loved her. "Really?"

"She never seemed right for you. I knew something was off with that one."

"Well Kora is a lot different from Andrea. I'm sure you would like her."

"I already do. She has my boy nervous as hell and I wouldn't have gotten to laugh as much as I did if it weren't for her." He joked.

"Really Dad?" I rolled my eyes even though he couldn't see me do it.

"I'm just giving you a hard time, son. I love you."

"I know, and I love you too."

"I hope your date goes well. Call me if you need any more pointers."

"I will. Bye Dad."

"Bye." I hung up the phone first. I sat there and thought about what he said.

"Somewhere special." I said to myself out loud. "We met at school. How is that somewhere special?" Suddenly it was like a light bulb went off in my head. I had the best idea yet.

It took some convincing, but I knew I couldn't have done this without my mother's help. After begging her I needed her help and promising I would explain everything to her about Andrea and me after my date with Kora. When she finally agreed I was ecstatic. My mom loved my idea and called us an Uber, so I didn't have to drive the whole way. This plan wasn't going to work at all if she didn't get there before I did.

I knocked on Kora's door nervously. I had sent her a text message earlier telling her to dress casually. I wanted her to be comfortable. I wanted this to be the best night of her life. Something she would never forget.

Kora opened the door in a black dress that hugged her body showing every curve that I hadn't noticed before. I had to pick my jaw up off the floor. I was speechless. Her black hair had curls in it, and her face had light make-up. I had never seen her wear make-up besides dark eye liner, but this time it wasn't so dark. She looked like a normal girl. Not so goth. She still wore her million bracelets on her wrists, but I was okay with that. That's what made Kora, Kora. I didn't want her to change although this new look on her was just as beautiful.

"You look amazing," I finally blurted out. Her face grew red as she blushed.

"I'm not overdressed, am I?" she looked down at her outfit. "I know you said casual, but this was all I could find that was casual."

"It's perfect. You're perfect, Kora." I wanted to grab her and kiss her right then and there, but I held myself back. "Our car is here if you're ready to go?"

"Yes, of course." She closed her front door and locked it. I reached for her hand and led her to the back passenger door. I opened her door for her and waited for her to get in. The smile on her face meant everything to me at that moment. I wanted to make her happy. I climbed in on the other side and shut the door.

"You have our destination, correct?" I asked the driver.

"I do." He replied simply.

I was nervous the entire ride. We barely spoke to each other. I could tell that Kora was nervous as well. We finally pulled up to the lake. Kora had a confused look on her face. She didn't understand why we were there.

"I wanted our first date to be where we first kissed." I confessed to her.

"That is so sweet." She said as she blushed.

"You don't mind right?" I asked, hoping she wouldn't.

"Of course not." Her smile assured me. "I think this is perfect."

"Well, you haven't even seen anything yet." I told her and reached into my pocket to grab a blindfold. I held it up in the air so she could see it.

"You're kidding me, right?" she didn't seem amused.

"Do you trust me?" I teased.

"Yeah but, is that necessary?" she asked.

I thought about it. It wasn't really but I wanted her to wear it anyways. "It is very necessary." I lied.

Kora made a pouty noise but turned her head so I could tie the blindfold over her eyes. Just then my phone dinged. It was a message from my mom telling me everything was set up and ready for us. I grew even more anxious. I hope this night will be perfect for her.

"Stay still. I'm going to get out and come around to help you." I told her. She did as I said. I opened the back passenger door and grabbed her hand. I slowly held her hand as she climbed out of the car. I told the Uber to wait there for a minute and he nodded his head. I slowly led Kora to where my mom was waiting for us. On the beach my mom had placed a small table with two chairs for us to have dinner. Around the table there were tea candles already lit and my mom added a walkway with them as well. It looked really cool, and I just knew Kora would love it as soon as she saw it.

"Can I take this thing off yet?" she asked. Without responding I started to untie the blindfold. Kora gasped and brought her hands to her face. Her eyes started to mist over. I knew this would be a date she would never forget. "This looks so amazing, Krystian. I can't believe you did this for me."

"I can't take all the credit. My mom helped setting everything up." I confessed.

"But it was completely his idea." My mom added. She smiled at us and walked up to Kota with her hand outstretched. "I'm Krystians mother."

"I'm Kora," Kora shook my mom's hands. "It's nice to meet you."

"It's nice to finally meet you as well." My mom smiled at her then looked at me. "Here are the keys to my car. I will take the Uber home. Mom placed her keys in my hand and gave me a wink.

"Thanks, mom, for all your help." I told her.

"Anything for my boy." She smiled, looking at me a little too long. "You two have fun and enjoy dinner."

Kora and I both waved bye to my mom as she walked off to the Uber that was still waiting.

"I can't believe you did all this for me." The smile plastered on Kora's face was even bigger than before.

"You deserve it. You're my girl now and I want you to feel special every day."

Kora put her head down and started looking at her feet.

"Did I say something wrong?" I asked hoping I didn't say anything to offend her.

She quickly looked back up at me. "No, not at all." She assured me. "If anything, you are saying all the right things. I'm just not used to it and not sure this is real."

"Real?" I was confused. "What do you mean real?"

"This just all feels like a dream to me." She said as she smiled at me. "Like I'm living some fairytale or something."

"This is definitely real." I assured her. "Let's eat before the food gets cold."

"Okay," she said happily.

On the table was a box of pizza and two plates placed in front of both seats. "I hope you don't mind, but I figured pizza would be okay since that's what we ate when we first spent the day together."

"It's fine. I love pizza."

"I love pizza too." I said to her as I grabbed a slice out of the box and placed it on her plate. Then I did the same for myself. "We also have some drinks." I mentioned. "Dr. Pepper or Coke?"

"Dr. Pepper." She replied.

I reached into the small cooler that was placed under the table. I grabbed two Sr. Peppers and the two plastic cups my mom had placed with them. I scooped what little ice into the cups from the cooler and filled both cups with the soda before handing Kora her drink. "I'm sorry if this date feels cheap." I kind of felt embarrassed for having plastic cups and a cooler. Now that I thought about it, this whole date felt cheap.

"Cheap? What are you talking about?" she looked offended.

"I'm sure you've been on plenty of fancy dates, and this is probably nothing compared to the rest you've been on."

"You're right." She replied. I felt my heart sink. What the hell was I thinking this was a good idea. This isn't romantic at all.

"This is nothing compared to any date I've been on because I've never been on a date."

I was shocked by her confession. "Are you serious?" I asked.

"I haven't. And honestly, I would have enjoyed sitting on your couch watching a movie or just hanging out at the park. Don't get me wrong, tonight has been amazing and you're amazing. As long as we're together I don't care what we are doing. You don't have to impress me, Krystian. I'm already yours." She explained.

I felt my body relax as I let out a sigh of relief. Kora didn't seem hard to please. Or maybe she was just going with the flow? Andrea would have wrung my neck if I had taken her to get pizza on our first date. She loved the flashy places and living in a small town we didn't have anything fancy. I remembered my mom having to drive over an hour to get to the restaurant for our first date. I think Kora is the match for me.

I looked into her grey eyes and smiled. "You don't know how much you just said means to me."

"What do you mean?" she asked.

"I'm yours," I repeated what she said. She smiled and her cheeks grew a little pink.

"I'm happy that you asked me out." She admitted.

"I'm happy that I did too."

"I was skeptical at first to say yes."

Her confession came to me as a surprise. "Why skeptical?" I asked.

"Well," she hesitated. "I didn't want to be a rebound or just the person you were using to get back at Andrea." She explained.

"Why would you think that?" I was a little disappointed that she thought of me as that type of person.

"That was just the first thought that came into mind when you asked me." She admitted.

"You will never be some rebound to me, Kora. Andrea and I are done for good. I promise you that." I assured her.

"That's what I needed to hear." She told me as she looked in my eyes. Kora's eyes were so stunning. I swear I could get lost in them.

"Would you like to take a walk?" I asked her after we had finished with our pizza.

"I'd love to." Her face lit up. I quickly got up from my seat and grabbed her hand to help her up.

"You are such a gentleman." She said with a smile.

"I just want to be good to you." I confessed. I wasn't sure what I was feeling for Kora, but I knew it was something I have never experienced with anyone else. I wanted to see where we could go. What we could be.

THE NEIGHBOR

I held her hand as we walked along the beach. I carried a blanket in one hand in case she got too cold. "Do you remember that spot?" I pointed out onto the lake.

She covered her face with one hand. "How could I forget. That was so embarrassing." She laughed, and I laughed with her.

"It's actually really funny now that you think about it." I admitted.

"It is, but it wasn't then. Why am I so clumsy?"

"I like that about you, Kora," I told her.

"Oh, it can get bad." She confessed. "Really bad." She chuckled.

"Then we'll laugh together about it." I promised her.

"Look the sun is about to set." She pointed to the sky.

"Shall we sit down and watch it again?"

"Sure," she replied.

I laid the blanket on the ground and we both sat down on it. Kora couldn't get too comfortable due to wearing a dress. She leaned back, holding herself up with her hands and her legs stretched out. We sat there in silence as the sun started to go down. As she watched the sunset, I couldn't take my eyes off her.

"It's so beautiful," she said still staring up at the sky.

"Yes, you are." I replied to her. She looked at me and I grabbed her and kissed her before she could say anything. I couldn't hold myself back anymore. I had to have her if she'd have me. She pushed me back and I felt disappointed.

"Unzip me," she said.

I thought about the first time I tried to make a move on her. I didn't want her to do something she wasn't ready for. "We don't have to if you're not ready."

"Unzip me," she said again. I did as I was told and before I knew it, we were back to making out as she was on top of me.

Chapter Eighteen

Kora

We laid on half the blanket and wrapped ourselves with the other end. Krystian held me close and tightly to him. I was feeling so many things at once that I've never felt before. My back was towards Krystian's chest, and he softly caressed my arm as we laid there in the dark with the moon being our only light.

"What are you thinking about?" he asked.

"So many things," I told him.

"Penny for your thoughts?" he asked.

"Is this really real?" I asked, still in disbelief.

"Is what real?"

"You and me? Us?" I explained.

"As real as it gets." He said before kissing my shoulder softly. I giggled as it tickled a little. "I want to kiss you all over." He began kissing my arm as I begged in laughter with protest, his warm breath hitting my skin. It tickled me. I began to laugh harder as he continued to further down my arm, which I believe made him more eager to do it.

"Okay! Stop!" I pleaded.

"I don't think so." He replied playfully. He made it to my wrist and stopped. I finally had the chance to catch my breath. "What is that?" he asked concerned.

"What is what? My bracelets?" I answered, not sure what he was talking about.

"Are those scars on your wrist?" He sounded upset. I tried my best to hide them with the bracelets. I could easily lie to him, but I didn't want to start this relationship off with a lie. I would feel guilty every day and he would eventually see them one day. I had to be honest with him no matter how scared I was.

I felt ashamed. I took a deep breath and let out the truth. "Yes, but it was a long time ago." I admitted.

"Are you okay now?" his voice sounded sincere. Something I've never heard before when it came to the scars on my wrist.

Most people would just avoid me. I wasn't sure how he would handle it. When my parents first saw them, my mom claimed I was just trying to get attention. She never saw it as a cry for help. Krystian being calm and not running away made me sigh with relief. He pulled my arm up to his lips and gently kissed the scars on my wrist. That was the moment I fell in love with him. He was everything I had always dreamed of. I was never going to let him go without a fight.

After an amazing evening with Krystian he walked me to my doorstep and kissed my forehead.

"I can't wait to do this again with you." He confessed.

THE NEIGHBOR

"Me either," I smiled, smitten by his words.

"Can I call you later?" he asked.

"Of course, you can." I assured him. "You can call me whenever you want to." I realized how desperate I sounded after saying that.

He smiled and revealed his dimples. They were the cutest thing about him. "I'd better get home before my mom starts to freak out. We have a lot of talking to do." He said before kissing my forehead one last time before walking back towards his home.

I walked into my house with the biggest smile plastered across my face. I couldn't wait to get to my room to write about it. It was like a fairytale come true. I never thought in a million years that I would ever have been kissed let alone by a boyfriend. Krystian was gentle and charming. Even when he first talked to me, I felt something I had never felt with anyone ever before. I wish I could call Terra and tell her all about it. She would be so stoked for me. I could already see us hanging out in her room both with big cheesy smiles and her asking me for every detail of my perfect date with Krystian.

As soon as I got to my room, I grabbed my journal and a pen and began writing. Trying not to miss any details of this night, I imagined I was writing a letter to Terra instead of writing in my journal.

Dear Terra,

Tonight, I went on my first date. Krystian is the sweetest and most charming guy I have ever met. I just know you would love him. He blindfolded me when we got to the lake and when we got to the beach, there were candles lit all around us. It was the most romantic thing I have ever seen. Now I know what it must have felt like for the girls in all those romantic movies that I've watched. He made me feel special and beautiful. Like I was his everything. And this was only our first date. I have a good feeling about Krystian. I think he may be my happily ever after. He was so gentle with me. He even saw my scars and kissed them. I had so many emotions all at once. I didn't know how to react or even what to say half the time. I remembered what you had always said to me just be yourself and if that's not good enough for someone then they aren't good enough for you. I was myself tonight thanks to you. I really hope you can meet him one day and then you will see how perfect he is. I just know you are going to love him. I can't wait to tell you more about him. I'll write to you every day and tell you all the details.

Til next time

I closed my book and turned my body over onto my back on my bed still holding the book to my chest. I couldn't wipe the smile off my face no matter how hard I tried. Was this really real? Did tonight actually happen? Was I in a relationship with Krystian Lopez? I let out a low scream of excitement.

"KORA! GET DOWN HERE NOW!" I heard my mom yell for me from downstairs. My happiness erupted instantly. I jumped out of bed as I wondered what she wanted. What could I have possibly done now? I've tried so hard to get along with her, so I didn't have to hear her yell at me. I could tell by the sound of her voice she was angry. I quickly ran downstairs to see what was wrong. My mom and dad were both standing in the living room, looking at the television.

"What's wrong?" I asked. They both turned to look at me.

"What the hell are you wearing?" My mom looked at me disgusted. I looked down and realized I was still wearing the dress from the date with Krystian. Fear ran through my body like lightning. How could I have forgotten to change? How do I get myself out of this one? Think Kora! Think! They were staring at me like I had lost my mind.

"I was just playing around" was the lame excuse I could come up with. My parents looked at each other then back at me. Neither one said anything, so I assumed they bought the lie.

"Did you have anything to do with this?" Mom pointed at the television with the remote as she changed the subject. I looked at the screen and it was breaking news that a teenage boy was found beaten to death. His identity hadn't been released yet.

"Why would you think I did that?" I was sickened that my own mother would accuse me of something like that.

"We all know what you are capable of." My mom said angrily.

"Now Helen, you said you weren't going to accuse her. You said you were just going to ask her about it." My dad came to my defense.

"I can feel it in my gut that she had something to do with this." She looked at my dad then back at me.

"I can't believe you right now Mom!" I shouted. "I'm not the monster that you think that I am." I began to cry.

"Oh, dry those tears," she demanded. "Nobody fell for them then and we damn sure aren't falling from them now."

"Helen, stop it!" My dad grabbed my mother's arm and turned her to face him.

"Let go!" She ordered as she jerked her arm from him. "You are always babying her. How is she ever going to learn?" My mom walked towards me slowly with her index finger pointing at me. "If we have to move again because of you I swear..."

"You swear what?" I said before she could finish her sentence. "Are you going to lock me up?"

"Helen please, stop." My dad begged her. "You are taking this too far."

"Too far?" My mom scolded him. "We know what she has done in the past and we both know she is capable of doing it again."

"It was an accident!" I shouted at her. "When are you going to start believing me of what really happened that day? I needed you! I needed you both and you both just turned your backs on me and threw me under the bus." I cried out. I just couldn't take any more of my mom's blame game. My dad thought whatever she told him to. He was too scared to think for himself because he was scared, she would leave him. "I am your daughter!

When are you going to take my side? When are you going to actually listen to me?" I hadn't realized that I was screaming at them, and tears fell uncontrollably down my face. I couldn't hold it in any longer.

They both just stared at each other for a minute then looked back at me. I waited for one of them to say something but neither one did. I rolled my eyes at them, and I ran towards the front door.

"Where do you think you're going?" my mom yelled after me, but I didn't dare to stop or look back at her.

I ran for what felt like miles until I couldn't run anymore. My stomach was hurting, and my legs began to feel like jelly as it became harder to breathe. I found some trees and decided to rest on one of them. I sat down and started to feel sick in the pit of my stomach. How did my day turn to this? It had been so magical and now it was a disaster. I didn't want to go home. I never wanted to see my parents again. I hated them for not believing me. For taking Tommy's side over their own daughter. I pulled out my pocketknife that I had placed in my shoe. I started carrying one since Andrea attacked me. Let her try that again and she'll regret it. It was my new safety net. I slowly opened it up and slid my finger across the blade. A small trickle of blood came flowing out. The sight of it excited me. I grabbed the blade and made three small cuts on my wrist. Blood grew more and more. I could finally feel something other than numbness. I felt alive. As my breathing slowly got better, I drifted into that night once more. That night my life would change forever.

"We have to get out of here." I told Terra. She stood beside me, shaking and scared. I didn't blame her. I was too. One of us had to be the strong one and get us out of this situation. I peeked around the corner, and I didn't see anyone. I listened out for noises. Nothing. This was our chance to run before Tommy and his friends found us. I started to slowly walk around the corner, my eyes looking in every direction, making sure the coast was clear. Preparing myself to run as soon as we saw anyone or even heard a noise. I felt Terra pull on the back of my shirt to get my attention. I stopped and looked at her.

"What are we going to do?" her voice trembled.

"Look over there," I pointed to our right. It was Marco's truck still running. I looked at her and she already knew what I was suggesting without having to say anything.

"Do you know how to drive?" She asked.

"No, but how hard can it be?" I answered. "We don't have to go far we just need to get out of here. We'll leave the truck somewhere they can find it. They can't prove that it was us that took it."

I thought about it for a second longer. It was the only thing we could do to save ourselves. It was risky but it was even more riskier sitting here trying to hide when we both knew they would eventually find us. "Let's go for it." I said, terrified. Terra grabbed my hand and we both looked both ways to make sure the coast was clear and made a run for the truck. We both climbed in on the driver's side, Terra first, then she scooted over to the passenger side. I put the truck in the gear that had an R and hit the accelerator. We went back fast and ended up backing into a car that was behind us on the street.

"What do we do now?" Terra asked in a panic.

"I don't know. What should we do?" I asked, hoping she had a plan. She was always the smart one. I started to panic when a short chubby man that looked in his forties climbed out of the driver side of the car that we hit. He was walking up to us, yelling in Spanish. I didn't understand what he was saying but judging by his tone they weren't nice words.

"Kora, look in front of us." Terra sounded horrified.

I looked and saw Tommy and the others running in our direction. My body froze up. My heart was pounding out of my chest. Sweat started to pour down my face and I couldn't concentrate. Tommy's nostrils flared out and his fists were clenched. There was no questioning it. He was going to hurt us badly. I had to do something but what? Think Kora, think. A bang on the window made me scream. The older chubby guy was at my window still yelling. I looked over at Terra who was trembling with fear. Her eyes were shut tightly. Her arm wrapped around herself as she rocked back and forth whispering something to herself. We had to get out of here. Tommy was almost to us. I had to protect Terra. I pulled the gear to D and hit the accelerator once more. This time we went forward. I turned the steering wheel to get us going straight. I almost hit Carmella, but luckily Tommy pulled her out of the way just in time. I saw them both fall to the ground. In the rear-view mirror, I saw Marco and Steve running after us.

Marco yelled something but I couldn't hear him. When they were finally out of view, I let out a big sigh of relief. I looked at Terra who seemed to have calmed down a little.

"Are you okay?" I asked her in a trembling voice.

She nodded her head yes. "What are we going to do now?" she looked at me. "They all saw us, and they will turn us in without hesitation."

"We ditch the truck, and we tell the police the truth. We had to get out of there Terra, they were going to hurt us really bad." I explained.

"I know, Kora," she said looking straight ahead.

"Everything is going to be okay," I promised her. I tried to smile, hoping it would ease her mind a little.

"Kora! Look out!" She screamed.

I looked back at the road and before I could do anything, a semi in front of us had slammed on his brakes, but it was too late. We collided.

I had woken up cold and alone. It took me a minute to realize I was still sitting against the tree. I left my phone in my room, so I had no idea what time it was. Are my parents out searching for me? I wondered if they had reported me missing.

"Yeah right." I said out loud to myself. Imagine them giving a crap about me. They were probably out celebrating.

THE NEIGHBOR

I returned home to find my parents in bed, asleep. I thought to myself how easy it would be for me to run away. I had to admit I was disappointed in them, but I knew this was going to be the outcome of it all. I went to my room and curled into a ball on my bed and cried until I fell asleep.

Chapter Nineteen

Krystian

I blew up Kora's phone after I heard yelling coming from her house. She never responded to me. Her mother sounded very angry, and I just wanted to make sure she was okay. I felt bad thinking that this was somehow all my fault. Did I keep her out too late? She never told me she had a curfew. I kept looking out my window into her room waiting to see her. I paced back and forth dialing her number once more. Straight to voicemail.

"Kora, please call me." I said in the message and then hung up. I was beginning to get frustrated.

"Krystian, you have to come see this." My mom yelled from downstairs. Her trembling voice worried me. Something had to have happened to freak her out like that. My concern went from Kora to my mother in an instant.

"Coming," I yelled back as I hurried down the stairs. "Aren't you going to be late for work?" I asked as I approached her in the living room. Her hands were over her face like she was mortified at what she was seeing.

"What is it Mom?" I was scared to even look at what she was looking at. Without saying a word, she just pointed at the tv.

I looked to see 'Breaking News' in big bold letters flash across the screen. A male reporter stood at the intersection of the 700th block of Luther and Lakeview, which was only a half of mile from our house.

"We have devastating news tonight. A young man was found beaten to death and left in the street." He began to say. "A mother and her two kids were on their way home when they discovered the body lying in the street, nonresponsive. Police are doing all they can to find the person or person's responsible for this heinous crime. The identity of the victim has not yet been released. Police are asking if you've heard anything or seen anything suspicious around eight o'clock tonight to please call them. With the anniversary of Kameron Lopez and Samuel Hernandez just around the corner, some believe the serial killer is at it again."

My mom gasped and I was still in shock.

"Who do you think it was?" she asked worriedly.

"I don't know. It could have been anyone." I replied.

By morning, the news about the murder grew like wildfire. In a small town like this, it was only natural. By the time I woke up, Mom had told me it was Rocco that was killed. I didn't know how to take it at first. Could it have been the same person who killed Kameron and Samuel? Couldn't be. Rocco and I were nowhere near friends, but I didn't want him dead either. My head was full of confusion. I couldn't think of anyone who would want to hurt Rocco. Everyone loved him. Well, besides me.

Kora and I sat on my front porch trying to enjoy the warm breeze. It was almost summer and the weathercaster on the news claimed it was supposed to be a hot one. I had a funny feeling that Kora was hiding something from me, but I didn't want to just blurt the wrong thing out. I still haven't gotten her figured out yet. I needed to stop being scared and just ask her.

"Where did you go last night?" I finally asked. "I tried calling you and you didn't answer."

"I was dealing with some stuff." She replied. I wondered what exactly she was dealing with that she couldn't tell me.

"So, you couldn't just text me that?" I asked upset. I knew she was keeping something from me, and it pissed me off that she was starting to act like Andrea. Was she ignoring me because someone else had her attention? After everything I did to make sure she had the perfect night she decides she wants someone else?

"I just needed to be alone." She responded. What was she not telling me? I could tell by the way she talked and her body language. I needed to know what that was without pushing her too hard for information. I wanted her to be able to tell me anything. She kept grabbing her bracelets and popping them on her wrist. She was just staring into the night like she was somewhere else. I kept watching her as she continued, and it was starting to get on my nerves. Then I noticed something. Her wrists had cuts on them. Not the usual scars, but fresh cuts. Cuts that weren't there yesterday. It was hard to see at first because the bracelets were covering them but once she lifted them up, I could see it. She told me she wouldn't ever do that again. She lied to me.

"Kora! What the hell is that?" my voice was louder than usual.

"What is what?" she looked up at me confused.

"This!" I grabbed her arm so she could see what I was talking about. She jerked her arm away from me and looked away.

"Oh, that's nothing." She lied.

"It's obviously something, Kora. Why would you do that to yourself?" I found myself angry with her. I didn't understand. I thought last night was perfect. Did she do this because of me?

"It's the reason I needed to be alone." She claimed.

"You can't do stuff like this to yourself." I yelled at her.

"It's my body and I'll do whatever the hell I want with it." She yelled back at me. "Nobody gives a damn about me anyways."

"I care about you." I admitted.

"For now." She mumbled under her breath. Why is she acting like this? What had happened since last night? Besides the news about Rocco, I couldn't think of anything else. She didn't know Rocco, did she?

"Why would you think that?" I asked confused. She ignored me and ran into her house. "Kora, where are you going?" I shouted to her.

"What the hell is she talking about?" I said to myself out loud.

"What is all this yelling going on out here?" My mom startled me. I didn't know she was standing behind me.

"Nothing Mom, you wouldn't understand."

"How about you give it a try?" she challenged.

"Not tonight, Mom. I'm tired." I said to her before walking inside and leaving her standing on the porch alone.

I could barely even sleep. I tossed and turned for hours. I was worried about Kora. Why would she do that to herself? Did she do it because of me? Did I do something wrong? Did she get in trouble for going out with me? I had to know what she is hiding from me. Why couldn't she tell me?

Chapter Twenty

Kora

Everything was becoming confusing. After the night Rocco was killed, it was all the town could talk about. My parents put up a donation box and Jen even donated all her tips to help the family with the funeral expenses. Every corner I turned someone was talking about Rocco. What a great kid he was, how funny he was. What a great athlete he was. How he winked at one girl, and she swore he wanted her. Crazy how when someone dies everyone seems to become your friend. I wondered how they would talk about me if I had died. Would they say how pretty I was? How friendly I was? Or would they even notice? They didn't even notice me now. But I'm sure after I died, I would have a school full of besties.

Walking the halls of Willow Creek High has become somewhat depressing. Now that everyone knew Rocco had passed away, nobody felt the same. I didn't know him personally. I just saw his interaction with Krystian. It wasn't a friendly interaction either. I kept my head down as I walked to my locker. Trying to avoid all the sad faces and some of the cries coming from not only students but teachers as well. As I turned the corner, I saw Krystian standing there. A smile formed on my face as soon as I saw him.

"Hello beautiful," he said smiling back at me.

I was flustered. I didn't know how to respond. "Hi," I said softly hoping my face wasn't as red as it felt. He seemed to be in a good mood.

"I've missed you?" he flirted.

"Really?" I asked like an idiot.

"Of course. Can I walk you to class?"

"Sure,"

Krystian grabbed my hand and began to lead me down the hall. "Wait there's something I need to do." We stopped walking.

"What is it?" I asked confused. Krystian grabbed me by my waist and pulled me closer to him. He kissed me hard. My body tensed up and I pulled my head away from his.

"What's wrong?" he asked concerned.

"Someone will see us." I stated as I glanced around to see if anyone was watching.

"I don't care," he replied as he leaned in to try to kiss me again. "Let them all see."

Krystian's warm lips touched mine and I couldn't resist him anymore. His tongue massaged mine and I was floating on cloud nine.

"You've got to be kidding me!" I heard someone yell from behind me. Before we could do anything, I felt a pain in the back of my head, and I was pulled around and slapped hard across the face. "What the hell do you think you're doing?"

I realized it was Andrea. She pushed me hard, and I fell to the ground.

"What the hell are you doing?" Krystian yelled at her. Her attention left me and went to him.

"I could ask you the same thing." She scolded.

"You dumped me, Andrea!" He told her. "Don't you remember that?"

"Yeah, I remember Krystian. But why her?" she crossed her arms waiting for him to answer.

"Because it's none of your business who I decide to be with."

"You know you miss me, Krystian." Her whole voice went from angry to sad. This chick was a real piece of work.

"What is wrong with you, Andrea?" Krystian asked her.

"I miss you." She said. She then wrapped her arms around his neck and tried to kiss him.

"Stop!" He pushed her away.

Before she could say anything else I jumped up and grabbed the back of her hair like she had done mine. My body was boiling, and adrenaline rushed through my body like it had never done before. I think I finally snapped. I started swinging on Andrea and she swung back at me. I couldn't even feel her hits, but I was hoping she felt all of mine. Before I knew it, someone was pulling me off her.

"What is going on here?" a man's deep voice asked.

"She attacked me out of nowhere!" Andrea cried out.

"She attacked me first!" I yelled.

"She's lying!" Andrea said.

"You are both taking a trip to the office." I had just realized it was the principal, Mr. Kurtis, who had pulled me off Andrea.

"I didn't do anything. Ask Krystian." I told him.

"Who?" he asked confused.

I looked around and Krystian was nowhere to be seen. Where the hell did, he go?" Why would he just walk off like that? Why wasn't he the one to pull me off Andrea?

"Let's go, both of you. I will be calling both of your parents."

I felt sick to my stomach as soon as he said that. I already knew my mother would overreact and blame me for it all. There was no convincing her I wasn't as bad as she imagined I was.

My mom was silent on the drive home. She was also silent when she came to talk to the principal. Andrea and I both had the chance to tell our sides of what had happened. There was no way I could tell my mom that Andrea attacked me because I was kissing Krystian, who is her ex, and she was just being a jealous whore. After Andrea said her side, I decided to just agree with her. Andrea's expression on her face looked shocked. Then suspicious. She didn't understand why I was lying. We both knew she was. I knew this was a battle I wasn't going to win no matter how the fight started. So, I gave up. I was hurting. Not from the punches by Andrea but hurting because of Krystian. Where did he go? Did he figure he wanted to be with Andrea and not me? Is that why he left?

We pulled up to the house and I climbed out of the car feeling numb. As I walked up the steps to the porch, I glanced up at Krystian's window. I knew he wasn't there. But something inside of me told me we were over, and it took everything I had in me not to start crying.

As soon as I walked in the door my mom did a complete one eighty. She slapped me hard across the face. Harder than Andrea slapped me.

"What was that for?" I asked as my eyes teared up. It was a stupid question and I realized it after I said it.

"What the hell do you think you are doing?" she asked angrily. I was too scared to tell her the truth.

My dad came running from the kitchen after hearing my mom yell. "What happened?" he asked concerned.

"Your daughter here is starting fights at school." She told him while looking me straight in the eyes. "We're going to have to move again, and we can't afford it."

My dad gasped. "How bad was it? Was someone hurt?" he asked frantically.

"It was a fight. It happens. Get over it." I told them. I was so tired of taking their shit and they constantly acting like I was going to ruin their lives or something.

"How dare you talk to us like that." My mother seemed shocked. "We do everything for you, and you will not disrespect us. Do you hear me?" her voice grew louder with each word.

"I defended myself just like I did in Phoenix. I don't care anymore whether or not you believe me. I'm your daughter and I'm tired of being treated like I'm garbage. I have to walk on eggshells around you both. When do I get to stop living in fear?" I felt the adrenaline returning to my body. I had to step away before I did something stupid again. I ran up to my room like I usually do without giving them a chance to say anything to me. I slammed my door shut and began crying hysterically. One mistake and I had to live the rest of my life in regret. One bad decision and I will forever be punished for it. Do they not understand that every day I wished it were me instead?

I remember waking up in the hospital, scared. I didn't know where I was, nor did I know what happened. The last thing I remembered was driving off in Marcus's truck. My mom and dad were by my side. But they were different. Their eyes were cold.

"Where am I?" I asked frantically. "What happened? Where's Terra?"

"You're in the hospital, Kora." My dad answered softly.

"Where's Terra?" I asked, scared to know the answer.

My parents looked at each other then back at me. But neither one said anything.

"Will someone please tell me what the hell is going on?" I demanded as tears fell from my eyes.

"You need to get your rest, Kora. It's already late and your mom is tired." My dad told me. I knew something was wrong. Why would they just leave me here? I'm their daughter. They should be here by my side. Why wouldn't they just tell me where Terra was? I just needed to know if she was okay or not.

"Tell me where Terra is before you leave!" I ordered them.

"She's here at the hospital, just on a different floor." My mom responded. Her voice was cold. I ignored it. I was just relieved my best friend was still alive. My parents didn't say anything to me after that. They just walked out of the room and left me there by myself.

The next day when my parents arrived back at the hospital, they told me that Tommy and Marcus were pressing charges against me for assault and for stealing Marcus's truck. I told them everything that happened, and I thought they were going to stand by me. I told them to ask Terra what happened. She was my witness, but they told me I was to never see her again. By the time I was released from the hospital they had already pulled me out of school. I ended up going to a detention center for six months. I tried calling Terra and messaging her, but she never responded. I knew she wanted to talk to me, but our parents wouldn't allow it. My parents took my phone away when they found out I had been trying to get a hold of her. I missed my friend, and I needed her now more than ever.

Chapter Twenty-One

Krystian

I felt nervous as the news crew were setting up. With the current events with Rocco's death, they wanted us to film in the school gym. My mom said they would ask us all questions about Kameron and Samuel, and we would all be sitting together like we were one big happy family after our losses. Debbie got to be included since she was Kameron's girlfriend at his time of death. I guess having someone there that knew Kameron as well as I did make me feel a little more comfortable.

My mom decided to help with my tie after watching me struggle for ten minutes. "I can't believe you don't know how to put one of these things on yet." She laughed.

"It's not like you taught me how, Mom." I didn't find it very funny.

"That's why you have a father." She replied.

"You divorced him remember?" I regretted saying it as soon as I did. My mom froze for a second. I could see the hurt in her eyes. I felt like a piece of crap making my mom feel like that once again. "I'm sorry."

She ignored me and finished tying my tie. "There you go. All done." She patted me on the chest and turned to walk away.

"Mom," I tried to stop her, but she pretended not to hear me and continued to walk off.

"Say something stupid again?" I heard a familiar voice say behind me.

I turned to see who it was, and my jaw dropped. "Andrea, what are you doing here?" She was the last person I expected to see here.

"I know things between us haven't been the greatest, but I wanted to show my support for Kameron and Samuel. I know you and your brother were close and I hate what happened to him just as much as you do. I loved him too." She said.

"That means a lot coming from you, Andrea." I was shocked at how sincere she was. "I appreciate you coming." After Andrea and Kora's fight, I figured she still hated me and wanted to claw my eyes out. I know for sure Kora did. I never got the chance to explain why I took off during the fight. I'm sure she didn't care what the excuse was.

"Not a problem. Don't be so nervous. You look good, Krystian." She said before winking at me and then walking off towards my mom. I watched her as she reached my mother. She got her attention, and she gave her a hug. A lot was going through my head. Andrea looked good. I missed her a lot. But I'm with Kora now and Kora is amazing. She has her flaws and I still think she is hiding something from me, but I think I am actually in love with her. I used to love Andrea. Maybe I still do a little bit.

The set-up crew placed chairs for us to sit on. There was a big lamp-like lights around us and a camera placed in front of us. The interviewer had a seat placed in front of us. Everyone started to take our places. I sat next to my parents and Debbie sat next to me with the Hernandez's on the other side of her.

"We are almost ready to begin." The guy behind the camera announced. I became even more nervous. The whole town was going to see this interview. Maybe even people outside of town. I took a deep breath and let it out. My mom grabbed my hand and squeezed it as the female reporter walked in. I had never seen her before. She was pretty for an older lady. Wearing a black blazer with black slacks to match and a white v neck silk dress shirt underneath. Her blonde hair was feathered back and reached her shoulders. Her make up was light so her wrinkles were noticeable the closer she got to us. Her blue eyes were bright. They made me think of Kora and how I wished I was staring in her grey eyes and not some stranger's eyes. I'd rather tell Kora everything about the night my brother was murdered and why he was. She would understand. Not this lady. She didn't know us. She was just here for a paycheck. My body started to get hot, and it was becoming harder to breathe. My mom must have noticed because she squeezed my hand a little harder.

"Breathe," she leaned in and whispered without looking at me.

"How is everyone doing?" the reporter asked as she finally reached us. She had a fake smile plastered across her face. I already didn't like her.

"Good," everyone said in sync.

"My name is Rebecca Collins and I'm a reporter for channel six news. I'm going to ask you all a couple of questions and afterwards you are free to say whatever you'd like." She told us. Everyone seemed to just nod their heads. I think they were all nervous as well. "Does anyone have any questions for me before we get started?"

"Who will all see this broadcast?" my dad asked.

"It will be broadcasted nationwide." She answered.

"Nationwide? Really?" Mr. Hernandez seemed shocked.

"Our purpose is to get Kameron and Samuel's story out to the world. If we believe that a stranger committed these murders, then maybe he confessed to someone, or someone knows something. It's good to get the story out to the world." She expressed. "Are there any more questions?" She looked at us all one-by-one waiting for another question, but everyone was silent. "Let's get started then." She looked down at the index cards she had in her hand. "Let's start by introducing ourselves." She looked at Hernandez's first.

"I'm Daniel Hernandez and this is my wife, Pilar Hernandez. We are the parents of Samuel Hernandez." His voice was shaky. Rebecca nodded her head and then looked at my parents.

THE NEIGHBOR

"I'm Hector Lopez. I'm Kameron's father."

"I'm Candice. I am Kameron's mother." My mom said softly.

Rebecca looked at me waiting for me to answer. I stalled at first and my mom nudged my shoulder to get my attention.

"Sorry, he's nervous, and he gets camera shy." My mom tried to defend me.

"It's okay," Rebecca assured us and smiled politely.

"My name is Krystian. I am Kameron's brother." I finally got the words out.

"I'm Debbie. I was Kameron's girlfriend before he died." Debbie didn't seem to be camera shy like me.

"Can you tell me what the boys were like growing up?" Rebecca asked.

"Samuel was shy. He had down syndrome. He was bullied a lot by other kids at school." Mr. Hernandez began to say. "When he was younger it was harder for kids his age to understand why he was the way he was. But he grew on a lot of people as he got older, and they started to understand him better."

"It was a struggle raising him. Nobody wanted to deal with him." Mrs. Hernandez chimed in. "Even as he was older, some still treated him differently because he was different. He was so loving and loved everybody."

"He sounds like a sweetheart." Rebecca said.

"He truly was." My mom added. "We loved seeing him."

"So, he and Kameron got along well?" asked Rebecca.

"Kameron loved him." My dad answered.

"Kameron was always so kind to him." Added Mrs. Hernandez.

It felt like we had been sitting there for hours talking about Kameron and Samuel. I was getting uncomfortable. I was agitated. They talked about their childhood and how they knew each other. Debbie talked about what a good boyfriend he was. And my parents couldn't pass up on how he was the perfect child. With all his good grades and the sports trophies, he'd won since first grade. How was bragging about him going to help find who did this to him? Question after question and I just wanted to stand up and leave.

"What do you all think happened to the boys?" asked Rebecca. I wanted to respond with something sarcastic, but I didn't. I kept my mouth shut like I did most of the time I was sitting here.

"I think Kameron was walking Samuel home and they were attacked. By whom, I don't know." My mom replied.

"It's just hard to believe anyone in this town could harm either one of them. They were both loved by many people throughout the community." My dad added.

"I think it could have been someone from here," Debbie added her opinion. "You can't trust too many people around here."

"Why is that?" Rebecca asked curiously.

"We are in high school. There is nothing but drama there. Kids get jealous over random things that aren't even important at the end of the day. I think someone here knows what happened to them and they are a coward for not saying anything."

"Wow," Rebecca's eyes grew wide. "So, you really think someone in your own community had something to do with this?"

"I do." Debbie replied.

"I hear there was another student that was just recently killed the same way Samuel and Kameron were. Do you think this murder was related?"

"Yes, I do." Debbie showed no hesitation answering.

My mom gasped with shock over Debbie's response, she was a fool to have not thought that already. It had even crossed my mind.

"Does this surprise you?" Rebecca looked at my mother.

"I guess I never really thought about it." My mom answered. "I guess once you step back and take a look, it does seem so."

"Do you all have anything to say to whomever it was who hurt your sons?"

"Just know justice will be served one day." Debbie answered before anyone else had the opportunity.

"Would the parents like to add anything?"

"I do," my dad said. "What happens in the dark always comes to light. We just want to understand why. These were two good boys who have never hurt anyone. Why did you have to decide their fate for them? They didn't deserve to die the way that they did."

"Wow, that was beautifully said. That's all for now. If there is anything else that we need, we will contact you all."

"When will it be broadcasted?" asked Mrs. Hernandez.

"We will have to review the footage and then edit it, so I think within a couple of weeks. Our producer will contact you with the information." Rebecca stood up from her seat and took the microphone from her blazer. The crew started disassembling everything around us.

"I hope this helps on getting justice for the Samuel and Krystian." Debbie mumbled under her breath.

"I hope so too." I said to her.

"I got to get out of here." She seemed jumpy.

"Do you need a ride home or anything?" I asked, just trying to be nice.

"No, I borrowed a car from my dad's dealership. I have to get it back before he notices it."

"Stealing cars now?" I chuckled.

"I said borrowed it, Krystian." Debbie didn't seem to notice that I was just joking with her.

"Oh, I'm sorry." I said as she walked away from me rudely. What was her problem? She had been acting strangely lately.

"Would you all like to go grab something to eat?" My mom asked the Hernandez's. "Our treat. We didn't expect this interview would have taken this long and we are starving."

"Sure." Mr. Hernandez accepted.

"Does Willows sound okay?" my dad asked.

"Of course." Mrs. Hernandez said with a warm smile.

My first thought was Kora. She was supposed to be working at Willows tonight. I could finally meet her parents and she can meet mine. I was anxious all of a sudden to hurry up and get there to see her. I knew she would be upset with me, but I also knew with both our parents there she would act casual. She hated confrontation. I understand why she fought Andrea. I didn't blame her for that. If she knew I took off for a test she would hate me forever. I had no choice but to get to class. I was on my last straw and if I didn't pass that test, I wouldn't be able to graduate this year. My parents were already bragging to family and friends about how proud of me they were, and I didn't want to let them down any more than I have.

"Can we leave now mom? I'm starving." I pouted.

"What is the hurry?" she asked.

"Kora is working at Willows tonight and I really want dad to meet her."

"Oh okay. Let's go then." She motioned her arm for me to lead the way. Mom and Dad were talking to the Hernandez's on the way out of the building. Crew members were still loading up equipment in the trucks.

"What is that laying in the road?" Rebecca asked as we met her on the front steps of the school.

"I'm not sure." My mom answered.

"It that a body?" my dad asked frantically. He then rushed down the stairs along with Rebecca and some of the crew members. I started to follow them, but my mom stopped me.

"Krystian, don't go. Let the adults handle this.

"But Mom," I pleaded.

"No, Krystian. Stay here." She ordered. I did as I was told even though I wanted to see what was happening.

"CALL 911!" My dad shouted to my mom. She hurried up and grabbed her phone from her purse and dialed the number.

"Krystian, do not move from this spot. Do you hear me?"

"Yes," I answered.

"Yes, hi, we need an ambulance at the high school." My mom began to say on the phone as she quickly ran to my dad's side.

I desperately wanted to see who it was. I'm sure my mom wouldn't notice if I walked up and took a peek. She looked distracted with what was going on.

Sirens from the firetruck and ambulances grew louder the closer they got to the scene. Everybody surrounded the body, so I made my way between two of the crew members on the other side of my mom. My dad was still kneeling next to the body. I couldn't see the face at first because my dad's head was blocking my view.

"What do you think happened to him?" asked one of the crew members.

"It seems he may have been hit by a car." My dad answered.

"We won't know anything for sure until the medics get here." Rebecca said.

"Here they come. Let's give them some room." My dad said to everyone. Everyone scooted back so the paramedics could get to the body. They had a stretcher with them. My dad stood up and started talking to the paramedics. That's when I saw him. His face was covered in blood, but I knew exactly who it was. It was Tyrell.

Chapter Twenty-Two

Kora

With two deaths, everybody was on edge. Everyone kept speculating and making up stories of what could have happened to Rocco and Tyrell. The thought came to me of Krystian being the murderer. He was the only one who had a real motive. Rocco hit him. Tyrell stole Andrea away from him. I couldn't forget the fact that he told me about the incident before Kameron was killed with Tyrell and Rocco. I had to admit it gave me chills just thinking he could have hurt anyone. He was so gentle and loving. I hadn't seen him angry. I quickly brushed the thought away. There was no way Krystian could have hurt anyone. Who else had a motive? Andrea possibly? There were speculations that she was involved somehow. The coroner said there was dark gray paint left on the body, so they were on the hunt for a dark gray vehicle. Not having any witnesses really put them in a bind. They definitely had their work cut out for them.

I saw Andrea sitting on the steps behind the school crying. She was hurting and I couldn't help but feel bad for her. I also knew I was the last person that she would want to console her. It was no secret that we didn't like each other. I set my bookbag in the step beside her and sat down. She looked up at me surprised it was I that was there.

"What do you want, Kora?" she asked hatefully as she wiped her tears. I took a deep breath. As much as I didn't want to do this, I wasn't the type of person to just leave someone hurting or try to kick them while they are down.

"You look like you need someone to talk to." I said softly.

"And you thought I should talk to you?"

"Well, you haven't got up and left yet." I pointed out.

Andrea rolled her eyes at me. "You wouldn't understand." She mumbled.

"Try me." I challenged her. "I know more than what you think I do. Even if you don't want to talk about it, I'll just sit here with you until you are."

Andrea didn't say anything. She didn't get up and walk away either. That must have been a sign that she really wanted to talk to me but just couldn't find the words to say. She placed her hands over her face and started crying again. I patted her back awkwardly. I sucked at comforting people.

"It's going to be okay." I said softly. Almost a whisper. Andrea heard me and looked up at me again. Her eyes were black from her mascara. She looked like a train wreck.

"You don't know that." She snarled at me. She was right, I didn't know that. That was a stupid thing to say. I felt like an idiot. I should just walk away before she makes me feel even more stupid. I grabbed the handle of my book bag but before I had the chance to stand up, she started talking again.

"It just really sucks, you know? Loving someone so much and then they're just gone." She wiped her eyes again. "Have you ever been in love Kora?"

I didn't know how to respond. Krystian was my first boyfriend, but I wasn't sure I was in love with him. Besides Andrea was his ex. That would make this situation even more awkward. "I don't know." I responded. It felt safer just to say that.

"If you don't know then you never were." She told me. I guess she was right. I never looked at it that way before. "I've been in love twice and they seem to keep being taken from me."

"I'm sorry for what happened to Tyrell..." I began to say.

"Why? Did you kill him?" Andrea blurted out. I could feel my face turning red. It got so hot I started to sweat.

"Wh... Why would..." I struggled to get the words out. Andrea chuckled at me.

"Calm down," she said. "I know it wasn't you that killed him."

How was she so sure? I mean, I know I didn't kill him either but why was she so sure that it wasn't me?

"There was a note." She said, staring off into space. It was like she read my mind and answered the question I was thinking.

"What?" I asked hoping she would repeat herself.

"There was a note. He received a note before he died. Just like Rocco did." Tears began to fall off her pale cheek once more.

"What did the note say?" I asked curiously. "Do the police know about it?"

"No, the police don't know because I never told them, and I don't know where the notes are now." She brushed the tears off her cheek. "The notes said, 'I know what you did'. Which doesn't make any sense because they didn't do anything."

"Why wouldn't you tell the police?" I was confused as to why she would keep evidence like that hidden.

"Because I thought it was just a joke at first. Someone playing games with us. Tyrell wanted us to keep quiet about it after what happened to Rocco, but I plan on going to the police. I have to tell them. Now Tyrell is gone. Maybe it would help find whoever did this to him." she cried.

I couldn't help but wonder if it had something to do with Krystian's brother, Kameron. "That's strange." I wanted to keep her talking. Maybe she could give me some clues or better yet even confess to it if they were the ones involved. "Do you have any clue to what it could have meant?"

"Are you listening to me, Kora?" her voice was starting to sound angry. "I just said they didn't do anything."

"I'm sorry." I felt embarrassed. I was going to screw this up. I just know I was. Just shut up and listen, Kora.

"That's why it doesn't make any sense. They weren't angels but they weren't bad either." She began to say. "They were just Tyrell and Rocco. I've known them both all my life."

"I heard rumors going around that they were bullies." I pointed out. I instantly regretted saying that after looking at and seeing Andrea's reaction to what I said. Her eyes squinted and eyebrows narrowed. If looks could kill, I would be dead right now.

"You didn't know them, Kora. I did. I don't care what Krystian has told you about them. He didn't like them because he thinks they had something to do with Kameron's murder." She stood up and spoke her mind.

"Did they?" I just came out and said it.

"I should slap you right now." She was offended.

"For asking?" That wasn't a good enough reason to slap me. At least I didn't think so.

"For being dumb. I loved Tyrell and I loved..." Andrea stopped herself. She took a deep breath and looked away from me. Why did she stop herself? Whose name was she about to say? Krystian? Rocco? Did she have a thing going on with Rocco as well? Maybe I was just thinking too much about it. I convinced myself she was talking about Krystian. She had to have been talking about Krystian and she stopped herself because I was with Krystian now. "Never mind." She finally said.

"Look I don't know what it's like to lose someone you are in love with. I did lose a best friend who I did love very much."

"It's not the same, Kora!" She shouted at me.

"I know that it's not. And I'm sorry I don't understand where your hurt is coming from. I just didn't want you to sit out here by yourself and cry alone." I tried to explain.

"You're not as bad as I thought, Kora." She said to me.

"I'm really not." I agreed with her.

"Look I'm sorry for everything, okay?" she apologized. "I should have never hit you. I was being dumb. I haven't been in love with Krystian for a while and he's a great guy. He deserves to be happy."

"I agree with you one hundred percent."

"Will you make sure he is happy?" she looked at me waiting for a response.

"Of course, I will." I didn't hesitate to answer.

"Don't worry about me trying to get him back. I'm not doing that again." She expressed. Her comment made me think she and Krystian broke up before. I was too scared to ask. We were getting along, and I didn't want her to yell at me again. So, I left it alone.

"Look I have to get going." I didn't want to, but I knew my parents would freak out if I came home after dark. I didn't want to tell her that. She would think I was a major loser.

"I'll walk you home." She offered. I was surprised.

"You really don't have to do that." I tried to tell her.

"It's okay," she said. "Krystian told me how strict your parents are, and parents seem to love me." She chuckled.

"Thank you I appreciate it." I responded happily. I wasn't expecting any of this to happen. If someone had told me that Andrea and I would one day be talking and getting along to the point where she was going to walk me home, I wouldn't have believed them. I felt positive about it.

"I just have to make a stop at my locker first." She voiced.

"No problem." I said in a chirpy voice. I was overly excited.

"Kora, you're being weird." She looked at me in a peculiar way.

"I'm so sorry." I told her embarrassed.

"Just calm down a notch, okay?"

"Yes," I responded fast.

I followed Andrea down the empty halls of the school. Most of the students were gone for the day except for the ones doing drama. They stayed later than usual today due to the deaths of Rocco and Tyrell. They wanted to add them to the tribute they were doing for Kameron and Samuel. A lot of changes had to be made on short notice.

Andrea stopped at locker 6505. I stood beside her as she unlocked it. I tried not to look as she put her locker combination in. I saw a group of students leaving the drama classroom. Several of them noticed that it was Andrea and I standing together. They looked at us awkwardly. I didn't blame them one bit.

"What the hell!" Andrea yelled out loud and got everyone's attention. "Did you do this?" she turned and looked at me. She had a red envelope in her hand with a piece of paper attached to it.

"Did what?" I was confused and now embarrassed because everyone was now staring at us.

"Did you write this, Kora?" she showed me the note and it read in red ink. 'I know what you did'.

"It wasn't me." I tried to convince her. How could she think it was me? I was with her the whole time.

"Stay away from me Kora or I'll tell Krystian who you really are." Andrea threatened as she slammed her locker door closed. She threw some books in her bag and stormed off. Students were watching us while whispering to each other. I felt embarrassed. Andrea humiliated me once again. I had no choice but to walk off confused and with my head down. Why would she think I wrote the note? Does it mean that she is next? She said Rocco and Tyrell got a note that said the same thing before they died. What does it mean? I had to find Krystian and tell him what I found out.

Chapter Twenty-Three

Krystian

I grabbed my flashlight out of my dresser drawer and flashed it through Kora's window. It was already night out, so I knew she had to be home. She opened her black curtain and waved to me. She pointed down indicating to meet her downstairs. I nodded my head and placed the flashlight back in the drawer after shutting it off.

I met Kora by the side of her house. As soon as she saw me, she ran to jump in my arms.

"I've missed you," she whispered in my ear.

"I've missed you too." I said before kissing her forehead.

"I have been meaning to call." She said. "I talked to Andrea today and..."

"Wait, you talked to Andrea?" I was shocked. "Is she okay? How is she handling all of this?"

"She's as expected."

"I just hope she is okay. I know this must be really hard on her right now." I admitted.

"I don't know what I would do if I ever lost you, Krystian." She buried her head in my chest. I wrapped my arms around her tightly.

"You won't ever have to worry about that because I'm not going anywhere." I assured her.

"Andrea said something to me that might help."

"Help what?"

"With your brother's murder." She said eagerly.

"What is it?" I was getting agitated. I wanted her to come out and say it already instead of beating around the bush.

"She said that Tyrell and Rocco got a note before they were killed." She explained.

"A note? What kind of a note?" she had my full attention now.

"She said it was a note that said, 'I know what you did.'"

"I know what you did?" I repeated. It didn't make any sense. "Did she say what they did?"

"No, she didn't, but when I walked her to her locker, she found a note saying the same thing."

"No way," I said in disbelief. "So, you think this has something to do with Kameron and Samuel?"

"It only makes sense."

"How?"

"You suspected Tyrell and Rocco having something to do with it. Someone is out for revenge. We just have to figure out who it is."

"Andrea didn't have anything to do with Kameron's death." I pointed out.

"Do you know that for certain?" she asked.

I was offended by her question. "Yeah, I know that for a fact!" I said rudely.

Kora took a step back from me. "I'm sorry if I offended you." She mumbled.

"No, I'm sorry," I apologized. "I shouldn't have said it like that."

"You still love her, don't you?" she blurted out.

I wasn't expecting her to ask that, and I hesitated to answer. I wasn't in love with Andrea. I was in love with Kora. She just wouldn't understand how I was certain Andrea had nothing to do with it.

"You don't need to answer that." She said before turning to walk away from me.

"Kora, wait," I reached for her hand, but I missed it. She ran into her house and left me alone standing in the dark. "What an idiot!" I said to myself as I walked back to my house.

As soon as I walked in the house my mom was throwing her purse over her shoulder. "Good, you're ready."

THE NEIGHBOR

"Ready for what?" I asked, not having a clue what she was talking about.

"We need groceries, and you can come help me." She replied.

"I don't want to go." I pouted.

My mom won the battle of me going to the grocery store with her. I hated shopping, especially with my mother. I wanted to stay home and try to talk to Kora, but the way we left things I knew she would still be upset. I had no choice but to let her have her space. Why did I have to say that? Of course, she would think I was still in love with Andrea. It was all my fault for her thinking that as well.

"Hey, Krystian," my mom stopped by the vegetable table. "Is that Kora's mom?" she used her eyes to show me the direction. She didn't like pointing at people.

"Yeah, I think it is." I responded as I got a better look.

"You should go introduce yourself." My mom said.

"I'm not so sure," I was hesitant.

"Why not? That's your girlfriend's mom. She does know about you and Kora, doesn't she?"

"Kora said she told her parents and I believe her, Mom." I wasn't trying to sound agitated but that's the way it came out.

"Then what harm can be done?"

"You're right," she convinced me. The smile plastered across her face let me know how happy she was to hear those words come out of my mouth.

I walked towards Mrs. Evans, nervous as I had ever been. My body trembled a little bit. "Get it together, Krystian!" I said under my breath to myself. As I approached her, she looked at me confused. She was reading on the back of a box. She casually looked around as if I was actually approaching someone else.

"Is there something that I could help you with?" she asked in a snobby way. This was definitely a bad idea. I should just walk away now. I turned to look at my mom and she smiled and nodded her head.

"Sorry, you're Kora's mom, right?" I got the courage to ask.

"Who are you and how do you know Kora?" she looked around again, only this time she was nervous.

"I'm Krystian," I reached her hand out to shake. "I'm glad I finally get to meet you."

"Is that name supposed to mean something to me?" she asked rudely.

Wow, Kora's mom was a piece of work for sure. "I hope so, I'm dating your daughter." I blurted out.

Her eyes narrowed and she pursed her lips. For a second there I thought she was going to claw my eyes out. "You must be mistaken. My daughter isn't dating anybody." She smiled and started to walk off.

"Kora Evans?" I said to her. She stopped and turned back to look at me.

"If you knew who my daughter was and what she is capable of, you would never look at her again. If you want to live, leave her now why you still have the chance." She said through her teeth.

"What?" This lady was crazier than I thought. What the hell was she talking about?

"I've warned you," she added before walking off again. This time I didn't stop her. I watched until she was out of sight. What did she mean if I want to live? What did Kora do? Did she kill someone? No way! Not the Kora that I know. Could she have? I needed more answers.

"So, how did it go?" My mom startled me.

"She was pleasantly surprised to meet me." I said without telling her what really happened. The last thing I wanted to do was freak my mom out with something about Kora that must have been lies.

"Is that a good thing?" she asked.

"Sure Mom, are you almost done? I'm ready to get out of here." I said changing the subject. I wanted to get far away from Mrs. Evans as I possibly could. Kora mentioned her mom being strict and difficult, but she left out the part where she was crazy.

On the way home we saw several cop cars, an ambulance, and firetrucks parked on a residential street.

"What is going on over here?" my mom wondered.

"I don't know." I said, trying to see between the cars. "Whatever it is it looks bad."

My mom rolled her window down to try to get a better view. We heard cries. Cries coming from someone that sounded familiar. It took me a few seconds for it to click on who it was.

"Andrea!" I yelled and unbuckled my seat belt.

"What?" my mom asked confused.

I opened the car door and my mom slammed on her brakes. "Krystian, what the hell are you doing?" she said in a panic.

I ignored her as I ran towards Andrea's house where there were several officers standing outside talking amongst themselves. I saw Andrea's mom on the porch, on her knees, with her hands covering her face. There was an officer standing almost in front of her. Andrea's brothers stood behind their mother, trying to console her as they were all crying. The closer I got to them; the louder Andrea's mother's wails were. The type of cry that makes your knees weak. I heard my mom cry those cries when she found out Kameron had been killed. The most painful cry a parent will ever have. You could literally hear her heart breaking. She just lost a child.

I reached the front porch where they all were. I was out of breath but didn't care. "What's going on?" I managed to say.

"Andrea is gone." Her brother said to as he wiped the tears from his eyes. "The policeman said she wasn't coming home."

I fell to my knees in disbelief. Not Andrea. It couldn't be Andrea. I found myself crying with her mother. I reached my arms around her and pulled her closer to me. She didn't resist. She squeezed me tightly and continued to cry.

Chapter Twenty-Four

Krystian

I watched the police pull up to Kora's house. So many thoughts ran through my head at once. Did she do it? How well did I even know her? Was her mother right? Nothing made sense anymore. I know Kora didn't kill Rocco because she was with me. As for Tyrell and Andrea, I wasn't so sure. Did she have help? Who else did she talk to in Willow Creek? I hadn't seen her associate with anyone besides Jen. Wait! Could it be Jen? Jen knows everyone in town. Maybe she helped her. I just couldn't picture Jen hurting anyone, let alone killing someone. She was a nice girl. Unless she just had everyone fooled. Like Kora had me fooled. I had to find out for sure. I tried to remember her friend's name. The one she told me about. Her best friend. If I could contact her then maybe she could answer some questions about Kora. Maybe shine a light on some things. Was she really a murderer or was her mom just a whack job? Ugh, what was her name again? Terry? Tanya? Terra? That's it! Terra. Terra Silva. Now how do I find her? She wouldn't be in the phonebook. I needed my mom's laptop.

My mom was in her room, reading a book. She didn't like it when I disturbed her during her 'me time' as she would call it, but this was urgent. I had to know now. Before someone else got killed. Or worse, before I got killed.

"Mom, I need to borrow your laptop." I said barging into her room.

"What's the emergency?" she sat up in her bed quickly.

"I just have some work I need to catch up on. Deadlines are coming up soon." I lied.

"I'll never understand why you always wait until the last minute to complete things." She said as she stood up and retrieved her laptop from her closet.

"Bad habit I guess." I admitted.

"You father and brother were the same way." She chuckled.

"That must mean it's in my blood." I joked with her.

She looked at me and rolled her eyes playfully. "Good excuse, Krystian."

I chuckled and turned to walk out the door until she stopped me. "Krystian, was that a cop car that I saw at Kora's place not long ago?"

I was hoping she didn't see them. I didn't know what to say to her. I didn't want to lie to her but at the same time I didn't know what was true and what wasn't. I wanted to know the details first. "Yeah."

"Does it have something to do with Andrea?" From the look on her face, I knew she was concerned.

"I don't think so, Mom." I tried to assure her. The last thing I needed right now was for her to flip out over Kora.

"How are you holding up with everything that is going on?"

"I'm doing the best that I can." I lied to her. I was honestly falling apart. I knew Andrea and I weren't together when she died, but she was a big part of my life for a long time. I never imagined her being completely gone. I always thought we'd still be friends or check on each other every once in a while. But not gone completely. I didn't understand why she had to die. She was no angel, but I knew she could never hurt anyone physically.

"I think you need to take a break."

"A break from what?"

"A break from life. I talked to your dad and we both agree you should stay with him for a little while. Get away from all this and clear your head." She suggested.

"I can't just leave, Mom," I was upset for her even suggesting it without asking what I thought about it first. "School is almost done, and Kora is here."

"Maybe Kora isn't right for you."

"What? You don't like her now?" I grew angry. I wasn't sure why I was defending her. I was in love with her but at the same time I hated her as well. I didn't have a reason to hate her yet. But soon I would know. If I can just get out of this conversation with my mom.

"I didn't say that Krystian." She pointed out. "You know what? Never mind."

"I'll think about it, Mom. Maybe for the summer?" I lied. I didn't want to leave Willow Creek. I had to tell her something so I could get back to what I was trying to do. Find out the truth about Kora. If there was a truth.

"Your dad would enjoy that." She said softly. I could tell by the tone of her voice that she was sad. I knew she was just trying to help me but right now wasn't the time.

"I love you." I told her.

A small smile formed on her face. "I love you too, son."

"I'm going to get started if that's okay with you?"

"Sure." She sat back down on her bed and picked up her book.

I rushed back to my room and waited for the laptop to power on. I was anxious to find out. It seemed to have been going slower than usual, or I was just in too much of a hurry? Finally, the home screen loaded up. I clicked on the search bar and then froze. What was I supposed to type in? I wasn't good at this research stuff. Andrea was always the one who helped me with my research papers. I went on a limb and typed in 'Terra Silva of Phoenix, Arizona' then hit search. So many articles popped up. 'Teen dies in crash', 'Family Loses Daughter in Car Crash', 'Driver of Vehicle That Ended Teens Life Does No Jail Time'.

I didn't understand what any of this was. This can't be the same Terra that Kora was telling me about. She made it seem like she was still alive, and she talked to her on a regular basis. I decided to click one of the articles to read the whole thing. Maybe I was looking in the wrong place. I had to have been. I clicked on the article that read 'Teen Dies in Crash'.

There has been one confirmed death on Friday's deadly accident involving a truck and a semi. 16-year-old Terra Silva has been confirmed dead after she and her friend Kora Evans (16) had stolen a truck. Kora was driving and did not have a license; the family has confirmed. Kora is in the hospital with minor injuries and the driver of the semi walked away with no injuries. We will update the story when there is further information in the investigation.

My heart sunk when I read Kora's name. She killed her best friend. How could she pretend she was still alive? It was an accident. It wasn't like she did it on purpose. Why would her mom warn me if it was an accident? I read through a couple more articles just in case I was missing something. I learned Kora was locked up in a juvenile center for six months. She was in the hospital for a couple weeks with a broken arm and leg. The kid whose car she stole said a lot of bad things about her. How she was a liar and manipulative. He said he believed she killed her friend on purpose. He was just trying to be her friend and introduce her to his friends, and she just stole his truck after Terra begged her not to. That didn't sound like the Kora that I knew. She was shy and gentle. A little mysterious, yeah. The way she talked about Terra I just knew she couldn't have hurt her on purpose. I just knew.

I closed the laptop and sat on my bed for a while, thinking. Do I tell Kora that I knew her secret? How would she react? I had been trying to call and text her, but she hadn't responded to anything. I heard her fighting with her parents a couple of times. I didn't know what about. I somehow felt a little closer to her now. Like I understood her better. I just hope she will feel the same. I looked out the window and I saw the police car had already left. I saw Kora in her room. She looked like she was writing. The police must not have had anything to arrest her. I doubt she did anything wrong.

I needed to see Kora. I needed to speak to her. If I told her my secret, then maybe she would trust me more. Maybe it will bring us closer together. It was Saturday and I knew her parents went out every Saturday evening. Kora never went with them. That was always our time to hang out with each other. I sat back on my bed trying to figure out a way to get Kora to talk to me. I knew it wasn't going to be easy. Especially since she had been ignoring me.

My mind ended up wandering off. I thought about Kameron and what he would be saying to me right now. I wondered if he would like Kora. I could see her and Debbie getting along. Debbie. I sat straight up in bed. Why didn't I think of Debbie? I had the perfect plan. I knew how to talk to Kora to get her to trust me, but I was going to need Debbie's help. I grabbed my phone and sent Debbie a message saying I needed a favor. It didn't take her long to respond. I knew she would help me with whatever I needed. I was happy I finally figured out a way that Kora and I can be together.

Chapter Twenty-Five

Kora

"Do you not see how stupid that sounds?" I was upset and I wasn't going to hold back any longer. "Rocco is three times my size. Do you really think I could beat him to death? I don't own a car. I don't even know how to drive. I was at Willows with my parents when Tyrell was run over. I talked to Andrea, yes, but that was it. You can't possibly believe I had anything to do with any of their murders."

"Ms. Evans, calm down. We are just asking simple questions. No need to go off the rails." Detective Robertson said. I rolled my eyes at her. "We just asked where you were on those particular nights."

"I was with Krystian Lopez on all the night's they passed away." I said not realizing my parents were still standing there and then instantly regretted saying that.

"You were with who?" my mother asked in a stern voice. I ignored her question. I was more scared of my mom than the detective. "Answer me right now, Kora!" Her tone got louder.

"I was with Krystian Lopez." I said in almost a whisper. I knew it was a lie, but I had to say something. I couldn't say what I was really doing. I wasn't sure he would collaborate with me, but it would buy me some time to come up with something better.

THE NEIGHBOR

"Can he verify that information?" Detective Robertson asked.

I nodded my head yes, but I knew Krystian couldn't verify anything. I didn't dare say another word in front of my mother. I could already feel her eyes burning a hole in my back.

"I will be in touch if I have any more questions for you." She looked at me and smiled. Not knowing that all hell's gates had opened because of her.

It wasn't a full minute after Detective Robertson walked out our front door that my mom lost it.

"What do you mean you were with Krystian the nights of all those murders?" she screamed at me.

I debated on just telling her the truth about our relationship. It was going to come out sooner or later. With everything going on Krystian was my only alibi. Well at least for Rocco's death he was.

"We have been dating for a couple of weeks now." I finally admitted.

"You went behind my back?" my mom asked in disbelief.

"I like him, Mom, and he likes me. I didn't think I needed your permission to have a boyfriend." I got an attitude with her.

"After everything you have done. You really think you deserve one?" she stated.

"Yeah Mom, after everything that has happened, I do deserve to be happy."

"Did you kill those kids, Kora?" she asked me without blinking an eye.

"No, Mom. I would never have hurt anyone." I began to cry. "For once in your life will you please listen to me and believe me?" I had had enough. I was so depressed because of her. Constantly blaming me for things I didn't do. How could my own mother think of me that way?

"It's just so hard after what you have put this family through." She began to cry.

"It was an accident, Mom. Terra was my best friend! Do you think I would kill her on purpose?"

"But they all said..."

"I don't care what they said. I'm your daughter. You should have listened to what I said. I was telling you the truth. They were going to hurt us, and we had to get away. I did what I thought was right."

"I'm so sorry, Kora." She apologized. For the first time in so long, she finally heard me, and she apologized. I didn't know how to react to the situation. Should I hug her? We haven't done that in a really long time.

"I'm sorry Kora, for lying to you about Terra at the hospital. I'm sorry for not defending you with those bullies. You deserved to be at your best friend's funeral to tell her goodbye, not locked up and lied to. There's so much I have been wanting to tell you, but anger has gotten in the way. I was heartbroken over it all. I thought if I was strict with you, then you would change, and I realized it was me who needed to change." She confessed. "I found your journal and your letters to Terra." She stopped talking and let out a cry.

"You what?" I was nervous of what she was going to say. My journal was personal and full of details of things I never wanted my mother to read.

"That's when I realized you were the one hurt. I constantly blamed you for ruining our family when really it was me."

"No Mom, you didn't." I didn't want her to put all the blame on herself. I knew I was responsible for the choices I made that day, but I had help with those choices.

I really missed Terra and it was hard for me to accept the fact that she was gone forever. She was cheated out of life, and it was partially my fault. I was the one who had to live the rest of my life knowing I was the reason why and the rest of them got off free with no punishment. My parents had to pay for what they had done. I knew we could have won all those cases, but it was my mom's choice to settle with them all. It almost wiped us out. She had to sell almost everything, and this was the cheapest place she could buy along with Willows. Luckily it was better here. Except for all the murders that were happening.

Out of nowhere my mom grabbed me and hugged me. I flinched. "It's okay, Kora," she said. "I'm not going to hurt you anymore." I could feel the warmth of her tears soaking through my t-shirt. She was being honest. My mom really does love me.

"What's going on in here?" My dad's voice interrupted us.

"Just a heart to heart with our daughter." My mom said as she wiped her tears from her eyes.

My dad looked a little concerned. He too didn't know how to respond to his wife's actions. It was all new to us. "Is it okay if I get a hug too?" he said jokingly. Although, I didn't really think it was a joke.

"Bring it in dad." We held our arms out to welcome him. He didn't hesitate.

"Things are going to be different from here on out. I promise." My mom promised us before kissing mine and my dad's cheek.

Chapter Twenty-six

Kora

"Kora, we are going out. Would you like to come with us?" my mom asked politely. I was still getting used to her being nice to me. After our little break through this morning, she was a lot nicer towards me. I didn't know how to take it at first. I thought it was just a big joke. Now I'm just going along with it hoping she is being genuine with me. I love my mom, but I wasn't so sure she loved me.

"I'm not really feeling good, Mom. I think I'll pass." I told her.

"Are you sick?" she asked, concerned. She placed her hand on my forehead. "You do feel a little warm."

"I'm fine." I assured her.

"We can stay home with you and just order in if you'd like?" she offered.

"It's okay, Mom," I told her. You and Dad have fun. Just bring me something back please."

"Sure, thing kiddo." She smiled, then kissed my forehead. "You have my number just in case something happens."

I dozed off in my bed after my parents left. There was a loud bang coming from my parents' room. I jumped out of bed startled. My room was pitch black but luckily, I knew my way around my room in the dark. I figured my parents were already back from their dinner. My stomach rumbled. "Just in time." I said to myself out loud. I flicked the light switch up and the lights brightened my room, almost blinding me. I opened my eyes and grabbed the door handle and opened my bedroom door to walk out.

"AAAHHH!" I screamed. "Who the hell are you and what are you doing in my house?" My heart was pounding out of my chest and my body was trembling. There in front of me, stood a girl. I think Krystian introduced her to me to her before.

"Why are you so jumpy?" she giggled.

Was she really laughing right now? This girl must be crazy. "What is so funny?"

"You are," she stated. "Why are you so scared?"

"Because a complete stranger is in my house, what do you think?" I didn't understand why she was being so casual. I'm standing here freaking out and she was pretending like we know each other or something.

"Calm down, Kora. I'm not going to hurt you." She chuckled.

I slowly was able to breathe again. I didn't know what her plans were with me or why she was even here.

"I just wanted to talk to you." She said simply.

"About what?" I was confused.

"I know you're with Krystian now and he deserves to be happy." She said, still smiling. It was a sinister smile, and it scared the hell out of me.

The girl began to walk closer towards me, and I slowly walked backwards. I felt my legs touch the bed. I knew I couldn't move back anymore. I had to think of something fast before she made a move. Think Kora. I looked to my left to see what I could find to defend myself. Nothing. I looked to my right. There was a brush on the dresser. If I could get to it fast enough. It wasn't going to hurt her or anything, but it was all I could see, and it was worth a shot. I pushed Debbie back and ran to the dresser and grabbed the brush. She lunged at me, and I threw the brush hitting her in her face. It didn't faze her at all. That was the stupidest thing you've ever done Kora. I felt like an idiot. Debbie grabbed me by my hair and threw me to the ground. I quickly climbed up and rammed into her like a bull. Her back hit my dresser, knocking everything off, then we both hit the ground. We tussled back and forth for a minute until she was on top of me pinning my arms down with her knees. I felt defeated. I couldn't move. She punched me in the face and the pain stung. Was she here to beat me up or kill me? Fear flowed through my body when I realized I was about to find out the answer to my question.

"Why are you doing this to me?" I cried out after she punched me again. Only this time I could feel the blood coming from my lip. Before she could answer me Krystian came running through my room and pulled Debbie off me. She flew across the room. He may have knocked her out because I didn't see her move right away. He grabbed my arm and pulled me up. "Are you okay?" he asked.

"I think so." I said, trying to ignore the pain in my arm. "How did you know to come over here?" I was so relieved he saved me before she killed me.

"I heard you screaming, and I had to check on you." He admitted. "What is going on? Why did Debbie attack you?

"She was trying to kill me." I began to cry. I had never met Debbie. Only heard Krystian talk about her sometimes when he mentioned Kameron. I just didn't understand why she would attack me if she didn't even know me.

"What? Why?" he was just as confused as I was.

"She said you deserved to be happy." I told him.

Krystian didn't say anything. He just had a confused look on his face. We heard Debbie moan and we both looked at her instantly. She slowly climbed off the floor and started rubbing the back of her head. She must have hit the wall hard because she left a hole where her head hit. How was I going to explain all this to my parents, who were probably already on their way home from dinner?

Debbie started to walk toward us.

"Stop her, Krystian!" I screamed, terrified of what Debbie would do to us. "She's the one who killed your brother and everyone else." I blurted out.

Debbie stopped walking towards us and Krystian looked at me. "No, she didn't." He said calmly.

"You can't be sure, Krystian. It all makes sense now." I tried to convince him.

"What makes sense?" Debbie was offended.

"She wants you all to herself and what better way to do that than to kill everyone, so they are out of her way?" I claimed.

"What are talking about, Kora?" Krystian looked at me confused.

"Yeah, what are you talking about Kora?" Debbie repeated him.

"You are in love with Krystian. That's why you killed everyone so you can have him all to yourself. Isn't it?" I accused her. "That's why you're trying to kill me now."

Debbie busted out laughing. "I was in love with Kameron, not Krystian."

"Kora, she didn't kill Kameron." He said again, only this time his voice was sterner.

"How do you know?" I asked him. He was in denial if he couldn't see what Debbie had done. It all made sense. Why couldn't I put it together sooner? It was all right here in front of everyone's face. "Why did she attack me then?"

"I didn't attack you!" Debbie pointed out. "You attacked me first and I defended myself." She wasn't lying about that. I knew that she was going to do something to me, so I had to take action first.

"Then what are you doing here?" There was no way I was going to let her lie her way out of this situation. And I knew she didn't have a good enough excuse to be in my room, let alone my house.

"Ask Krystian." She looked at Krystian, waiting for him to answer.

I looked at Krystian and he looked at me. "Well?"

"I told her to come over here," he said simply.

"What? Why would you do that, Krystian?" I was in disbelief. Why would he send Debbie to my house to attack me?

"I needed to talk to you both." He admitted.

"Talk to us about what?" I was furious with him. What made him think sending Debbie to my house was a good idea? Why not tell me about it? Hell, we could have met up at his place.

"You really thought not informing me was such a great idea?" I said angrily. "All this could have been prevented if you had just called or messaged me, Krystian."

"You're right, Kora. I'm sorry." He apologized. "But you haven't been answering my calls or texts."

I knew I had been avoiding him lately. After what happened to Andrea, I wanted to give him space. He seemed distant from me already. "I'm sorry." I apologized to him. "I should have responded.

"It's okay." He said before kissing my forehead.

"But that still doesn't change the fact that Debbie killed everyone." I reminded him.

"Maybe you killed everyone!" She blamed me before walking towards me. Krystian lifted his arm up to stop her. She didn't dare challenge him.

"Kora, shut up about that. I told you she didn't kill Kameron or Samuel. I know who did though." He yelled at me. I felt more hurt by him yelling at me than Debbie punching me. Maybe because he hit me right in the heart.

"Who?" Debbie was surprised and anxious at the same time.

Krystian looked at me and his eyes grew dark, and I didn't recognize him anymore. For the first time since I've known him, I actually felt terrified looking in his eyes. "I did."

Chapter Twenty-Seven

Krystian

"I don't understand. What are you saying, Krystian?" Debbie asked with a confused look on her face. I knew she was about to cry. That's the last thing I needed. Hearing her crying pathetically.

"I killed Kameron and Samuel." I repeated myself.

Both girls gasped. "What? How? Why?" Debbie asked, not believing I was telling the truth.

I debated if I should tell them my secret or not. "There was a party that night," I hesitated to confess but I knew I had to before anyone else got killed. "Kameron snuck out of the house to go to the party. I knew who he was going to meet."

"He came to meet me." Debbie was so sure of herself.

"Let him finish," Kora snapped at her. I chuckled at how cute she looked at this very moment. That little attitude made her more attractive than she already was.

"Go on," Debbie snarled.

"Anyways, I didn't go to the party. I waited until the party was over and I saw Kameron standing by himself and I knew I had to do it right then and there. No witnesses. It was dark out. He was intoxicated so I was going to make it look like he stumbled and hit his head hard enough to kill him. But that didn't go as planned. Kameron was a lot stronger than me."

I found myself going back to that night like it was happening all over again. I could smell Andrea's perfume still on him. He was looking at a bush like he had heard something. It was too dark to see. I picked up a rock and threw it hard, hitting his head. He didn't go down like I thought he would.

"What the hell?" Kameron cried out. Blood was dripping from the back of his head and onto his gray hoodie. Why he was wearing a hoodie, I didn't know. The weather was perfect. Not as humid as it usually is around this time.

Kameron grabbed the back of his head and turned to look my way. He realized it was me. "Krystian, what the hell are you doing?"

I froze up and didn't know what to say. I wasn't expecting him to know. I was expecting him to just fall dead. I stood there shaking not knowing what to do and before I knew it Kameron tackled me to the ground. We wrestled for a moment, and he would win easily. I never worked out a day in my life and he spent most of his time in the gym. I was a fool to think I could kill him. I didn't have the strength he had. Kameron punched me in the stomach repeatedly. It was becoming harder to breathe. I thought he was going to end up killing me instead. I looked to my right and saw the rock I had hit him with earlier lying close by me. I reached out for it, and he didn't even notice.

"Why Krystian? Why?" he begged me as he stopped hitting me so he could take a breath.

"Because of Andrea." I confessed. His eyes looked saddened. He knew he had done me wrong, and he knew he could never fix it.

"I'm in love with her," he said softly. My heart felt like it had exploded. I was in love with her. There was no way Kameron could love her. Not like I did. The look in his eyes were the same one that Andrea gave every time she looked at him. I saw the way Andrea looked at him. I could feel her pulling away from me. They talked a lot and she always wanted to do stuff that involved him. I did everything I could to make her happy. I failed. My brother stole the love of my life. I saw it but didn't want to believe it. How could they do this to me?

Kameron stood up and reached for my hand. I let him help me up. I was boiling with hatred. My body felt hot, and I could feel sweat starting to pour down my forehead. I wanted him to pay for what he had done. Pain filled my stomach from where he kept hitting me. I wasn't sure I was going to be able to finish him off. Just let it go Krystian! It isn't worth it. I thought to myself.

"Krystian, I am sorry." He apologized. I wasn't going to accept it. I hated him now. How could I ever forgive him? "We planned on telling you. We just haven't found the right time."

I just wanted to hit him again. He shouldn't be trying to find the right time to tell me anything.

"We both fell in love with each other. We didn't plan it." He tried to explain. "We didn't want to hurt you."

"Promise me it ends tonight!" I demanded him.

"Krystian, you're not understanding." He took a deep breath.

"What am I not understanding?" I wanted to know.

"We love each other. We aren't going to stop." Those words kept repeating in my head and I lost all control. I felt like I was someone else. Someone angry and dark. What did he mean they weren't going to stop? Andrea planned on leaving me? They planned on being together in front of me? I had to stop Kameron. I wasn't going to let him win. Andrea was mine and she will never be his. I gripped the rock in my hand tighter and I swung fast at Kameron's face. He fell after the first two blows to the head, but I jumped on top of him and just kept swinging. By the time my arm gave out, Kameron's face was covered in blood. I almost didn't recognize him. I stuck the rock in my pocket and climbed off him. As I began to walk away, I heard crying coming from the bushes.

"Who's there?" I called out, feeling nervous. Someone saw me. I couldn't get away with this if someone saw me. I started to panic. I walked slowly towards the bushes with adrenaline still flowing through my body like a lightning bolt. I pulled the rock out of my pocket. I was ready for whoever it was. Samuel fell out of the bushes onto the ground. He covered his head with his arms blocking me from hitting it. I had to do something. He saw everything and would snitch on me in a heartbeat. Samuel was fond of Kameron. Kameron was his hero. Like he used to be mine. I watched Samuel lay in a ball and cry. I almost didn't go through with it, but I knew I had no other choice.

"I'm not going to hurt you, Samuel." I said softly to him. He looked up at me scared and eyes puffy from crying. I reached my hand out for him to grab. He let me help him up. He believed me. As we started to walk away, I let him get in front of me and I did the same to him as I did to Kameron. I didn't feel guilty for what I did to Kameron, but I did for Samuel. He didn't do anything wrong. None of this was his fault. It was Kameron's fault.

"Kameron was cheating on me?" Debbie asked softly as tears began to fall down her cheeks.

"I'm sorry you had to find out this way." I told her. I knew she would feel the same way I felt when I found out. She loved Kameron just as much as I loved Andrea.

"That can't be true. Maybe you thought you saw something, but it wasn't really what you saw." Debbie tried to find every excuse for my reasoning to be untrue. She could try all she wanted but there was no other reason.

"I know what I saw, Debbie. I saw it more than once. I saw it several times and wished what I was seeing wasn't real, but it kept happening. Over and over again and it wasn't going to stop until I stopped it myself. Andrea was falling in love with him, and Kameron told me himself that he was in love with her." I tried to explain it again to her.

"I would have noticed if he was drifting away from me." She still was in denial. "I would have noticed, Krystian." She placed her hands over her face and cried. Kora still looked distraught but kindly placed her hands on Debbie's shoulders for comfort.

Kora looked at me confused. "Why would you tell us this?" she finally spoke.

"Because I know you won't turn me in." I admitted.

"What makes you so sure of that?" Debbie asked as she wiped her eyes.

"Because I know for a fact that I'm not the only killer in this room." I looked at them both with a grin on my face. They both looked at each other trying to guess which I was talking about.

"What are you talking about?" Kora finally asked, removing her hands from Debbie's shoulders and looking around nervously. I took a step towards them, and they both took a step back. I chuckled that they were both still in fear of me. I didn't blame them though. I just confessed to killing my brother.

"I'm not the one who you should be afraid of." I smiled at them both. "I know both of your secrets." I admitted. They both went from confused too nervous instantly.

"What are you talking about, Krystian?" Kora asked.

"I know all about your friend Terra." I confessed. I knew that hit a soft spot for Kora. Her eyes began to water, and her body began to tremble.

"How do you know about that?"

"I emailed her parents and told them I knew you and they had no problem throwing you under the bus."

"It was an accident," she cried out. "She was never meant to get hurt. I was trying to save her. You have to believe me, Krystian."

"I do believe you, Kora." I told her. "But what do you think this town would think of someone who has already committed murder? They would shun you and then your parents would lose Willows because of you. People started dying as soon as you came to town. Someone you almost got into a fight with."

"I didn't kill Andrea or the others," she pleaded. "You have to believe me."

"I do believe that. Debbie killed them." I blurted out. Debbie's eyes grew wide with shock that I knew it was her.

"What makes you think I killed them?" she tried to play it off.

"I admit you fooled me in the beginning. I thought it had to have been Kora doing it. That's why I started digging into her past. I followed her for a little while and did some snooping, but it led me nowhere."

"You really thought I could be capable of murder?"

"Well, again Terra." I pointed out.

"It was an..." she began to say.

"We know it was an accident." Debbie cut her off eager to know what I knew. "Back to what you were saying.

"I thought long and hard about it. They each received a letter before they were killed. Who would do that to them? I'm the one who killed Kameron, so it had to be someone who thought they were the one's killing them. You, Debbie, are the one who kept warning me about them because you were the one who thought they did it."

"I was so sure that they did do it," she confessed. "They looked guilty. I thought Kameron died protecting Samuel from them all."

"Are you trying to blackmail us?" Kora blurted out.

"Why would I do something like that?" I responded. "I just don't want you all snitching on me so if you can keep my secret, I will keep yours." I offered them.

"Deal!" Debbie didn't hesitate. "If I had known you were the one who killed Kameron, I would have never done what I did."

"Well, you did. I think you're making a good choice." I told her and then looked at Kora waiting for her response. "Kora baby?"

"Don't call me that." She snapped. I smiled at her.

"I get it. You are going to break up with me for this. I already had that figured out."

"What I did was an accident. If I was going to go to jail for it, then I would have been arrested."

"True, but" I paused to look at the scared reaction on her face. "I'm sure Debbie and I can convince the police that you are the one who killed everyone. That's two against one. It's not that hard to feed them evidence pointing the murders towards you."

"Why would you do that to me?" Kora looked at me and Debbie both.

"We can't go to jail." Debbie told her. I knew she was on the same page as I was. "I'd tell them you told me how much you hated Andrea and wanted Krystian all to yourself."

"But that's not true." Kora cried out.

"Who is going to believe the new girl?" I told her. "The mysterious new girl filled with secrets." I added.

"I can't believe you would do that to me. I thought you liked me."

"I do like you, but this isn't about liking someone. This is about not getting caught." I walked slowly towards her. Kora was trembling. I knew I had her right where I wanted her.

"And if you can't keep our secret then we'd have to kill you as well." Debbie added.

"I'll keep it." Kora put her hands in front of her showing she didn't want us to get any closer to her. "I won't tell anyone, I promise."

"Good choice." Debbie said in a giddy tone.

"You both have to stay away from me from now on. Don't talk to me and don't act like you know who I am. I am invisible to you both." Kora said seriously. I felt my heart sink to my gut. I wasn't so sure I could keep that promise. But I knew I had no choice.

"Okay, that should be easy enough. You have always been invisible to me. If it wasn't for Krystian, I would have never known you existed." Debbie had no problem to Kora's proposal.

"Are you sure that's what you want, Kora?" I asked. I guess it would only make sense that she wouldn't want to be with me anymore. Maybe deep down I still had a little bit of hope. I liked her a lot, but I know the circumstances are different now. Kora nodded her head. I felt a little disappointed. She was going to keep our secret and I wasn't going to ask anything else of her.

"So, we have a deal?" Debbie asked and placed her hand out for Kora to shake.

Kora hesitated at first, but then shook Debbie's hand. "If any of you get caught, please leave me out of it." Debbie and I both agreed. "Now will you both get the hell out of my room? My parents will be here any minute now.

Debbie walked out of the room, and I slowly walked up to Kora. "Please leave, Krystian." She said to me as she walked to the door and held it open for me. I wanted just one last kiss from her. I wanted to feel her lips just one last time. I brushed her face softly and she pulled her face away from me. That's when I dropped the good guy act. I was tired of pretending who I was. It was Kora's turn to meet the real me. I chuckled. She was going to give me what I wanted. I knew she would never turn me in. Kora was weak. I had all the control over her. I grabbed the back of her head and pulled her towards me. I kissed her hard. She didn't resist either. When I was finally done, I opened my eyes to see Kora staring at me with tears in her eyes.

"We are done when I say we are done." I warned her.

"Leave me alone, Krystian, please." She begged.

"I'll leave you alone for now, but just know I'll pop up when you least expect it. Could be a year, maybe five years. Hell, it could be tomorrow, and we can act like today never took place, but we aren't done until I say we are done."

"Krystian, you are a psycho."

I chuckled. "Yeah, that's what I've heard." I said to her as I walked out of her room. "See you later, neighbor." I waved. Kora slammed her bedroom door shut. I could hear the click of her locking it. I grinned knowing I had her right where I wanted her. Kora will always be mine.

Chapter Twenty-Eight

Kora

Ten Years Later

The smell of bacon and eggs awoke me from my sleep. My husband must have been making breakfast for the kids. We have been married almost five years now and have two daughters, ages two and four. My life has changed completely since the night Krystian confessed to murdering his brother. I just didn't have it in me to continue to stay with him. Actually, he scared the hell out of me. He was different. He wasn't the same boy I had fallen in love with. He was more controlling and manipulative. He promised me he was never going to let me go. Things got really bad during the summer, and I had to beg my mom and dad to let me go to college sooner. They hated the fact that I left early, and we didn't get to finish our summer plans. Debbie would come around and torture me as well. I think Krystian put her up to it. They both had a goal to make my life a living hell.

I kept Krystian and Debbie's secret. I haven't even told my husband, Brent, and I regret it every day. I was so scared of my parents losing everything again and I didn't want them to go through that again because of my poor actions the night Terra passed away. Now they can't even see their granddaughters unless they make the trip to see them. They try to tell me all the gossip from Willow Creek, but I try not to listen.

I walked down the stairs to meet my family in the kitchen. Two beautiful faces ran to me ecstatic that I was finally awake. I gave them a hug as they wrapped their arms around my legs, squeezing them hard. My husband chuckled at the sight of us.

"Chloe, Britney. Let Mom go. Breakfast is done." Brent announced.

"Girls, let's help Daddy set the table." The girls were full of energy as they ran to the counter and grabbed the silverware out of the drawer. Brent was carrying two plates with eggs and bacon. He leaned in to give me a kiss. My life felt like it was a movie or something. My heart was complete now. I just stared off at my family as they set the table. Krystian was the first guy I ever fell for and when Brent asked me out in college, I was scared to let him get close to me. After a year of talking and hanging out I finally agreed to date him, and I haven't regretted it once. He was an amazing man. He took good care of me and our daughters. I didn't know what I would do without him.

A knock on the door disrupted everyone's focus. "Will you get that, honey?" Brent asked as he sat our youngest daughter Britney in her highchair.

"Sure," I told him as I looked at my happy family again before going to retrieve the front door. "Who could this be?" I wondered as I reached the door handle. There was another knock before I had turned the knob.

THE NEIGHBOR

"Hold on." I hoped they had heard me. I opened the door now curious about who it could have been. My eyes grew wide, and my jaw dropped. My heart started racing at the speed of light. Almost looking the same as he did back then. He smiled at me. A sinister smile. A smile I swore I never wanted to see again. I knew he was only here to demand something of me.

I tried to speak, but the words barely came out. "Krystian?"

Acknowledgements

Where to begin?

Of course, my three awesome daughters who constantly support my dreams and are patient with me. For their opinions, and critiques. I wouldn't be where I am today if I didn't have you three amazing girls in my life.

The family who has supported me from the beginning. Whether it had just been a congrats or a purchase of one of my books, you are all amazing and I thank you a million times. I hope I make you all proud. Love you all!!!

To my friends who have supported me in this journey. You all are the greatest. I wouldn't have come this far without you all helping me research, or your opinions whether they were good or bad. I'm forever thankful for you all!

To the fans I've made along the way. I hope you enjoy this story as much as I've enjoyed writing it. Thanks for your support in purchasing my books. Much love!

Don't miss out!

Visit the website below and you can sign up to receive emails whenever F. A. Witte publishes a new book. There's no charge and no obligation.

https://books2read.com/r/B-A-SOUM-HURHC

BOOKS 2 READ

Connecting independent readers to independent writers.

Also by F. A. Witte

Mine
Revenge
The Neighbor
The Fall of Jacintha

Watch for more at https://fawitte08.wixsite.com/fawitte.

About the Author

F. A. Witte was born in Fairview, Oklahoma. She now calls El Reno, Oklahoma her home. She has an Associates Degree in Medical Assisting but, writing has always been her passion. Starting out with poetry, then to short stories, and finally expanding to novels. She has always been a big fan of Poe, King, and Patterson. When she's not writing, working, or spending time with her daughters and grandkids, she likes to get comfortable with a good book from any genre.

Read more at https://fawitte08.wixsite.com/fawitte.